The Chicano War

The Chicano War

William Campbell Gault

Walker and Company
New York

First published in the United States of America in 1986 by the Walker Publishing Company, Inc.

Published simultaneously in Canada by John Wiley & Sons Canada, Limited, Rexdale, Ontario.

Library of Congress Cataloging-in-Publication Data

Gault, William Campbell.
The Chicano war.

I. Title.
PS3557.A948C49 1986 813'.54 85-22556
ISBN 0-8027-5640-9

Book Design by Teresa M. Carboni

Printed in the United States of America

10 9 8 7 6 5 4 3 2 1

For Art Scott
Connoisseur of Crime

1

It was Orlando Davis who conned me into the Chicano caper. Orlando is big and black and mean. He had spent six years with the former Oakland Raiders, now the Los Angeles Raiders, and several years in various penal institutions around the state.

As a major benefactor of the Tomorrow Club, which Orlando ran with an iron fist, I would drop in from time to time. The Tomorrow Club was founded by civic-minded people who believed that if the underprivileged kids in mostly over-privileged San Valdesto were given some attention, latent athletic, creative, or mechanical talents might be nurtured and the kids might wind up on the sunnier side of the law.

I had not been one of the board members who had voted for Orlando. An all-American boy like Roger Staubach would have been more to my liking. But the board was probably right; blacks and Chicanos would not be likely to accept a square, rich, and forthright whitey like Roger as a soul brother.

Still, as a man who had spent years among the seedy and the shiftless, I made it my duty to keep an eye on Orlando. And I got to like him—and so did the kids. At least most of them did. The harsh truth is that some kids, thanks to us, are beyond redemption.

It was after our regular Thursday morning workout on

the handball court, where I beat him for the first time in two months, that Orlando told me about Peter Chavez.

But he didn't start by mentioning Peter. He asked me if I knew Karl Kranski.

"I know who he is," I said. "I knocked him on his ass often enough when he was playing for the Dallas Cowboys."

Orlando smiled. "I'll bet you did. In your dreams you did."

"If you know him," I said, "you could ask him. What's he doing now?"

"Working for the city. He's a juvenile parole and probation officer. He came up here a month ago."

"From where?"

"From Los Angeles, from the L.A.P.D. He was on the street down there for a while. But he was a cowboy on the street, too. So they took him off the street and put him on parole and probation. And then he married money and came up here."

"And they stuck him into the juvenile division?"

Orlando nodded. "Chief Chandler Harris thought a famous athlete like him would be a model to the kids."

"A model? Kranski? The word I had on him, he was a womanizer and a barroom brawler in Dallas."

"That's the same word I had. But the chief is not a sports fan."

"I've noticed that. He thought I played basketball. If Kranski married money, why the day labor?"

Orlando shrugged. "Maybe he likes the action. Maybe he thinks it's sissy to live off a woman."

"It is," I said.

He shook his head. "Not if you believe in equal rights. Anyway, there is this borderline kid I'm working on, a kid named Peter Chavez, ready to go either way. He's the best damned mechanic we had in the shop here. He got into a little trouble a couple weeks ago and Kranski is really laying on the heavy hand."

"What kind of trouble?"

"He stole a car. Just one of those joyride deals. He left it as clean as he found it. I've got this hunch Kranski is a bigot."

I shook my head. "No way! He roomed with Jess Washington for three seasons and Jess is blacker than you are."

"Nobody," he said stiffly, "is blacker than I am. Maybe Kranski specializes in Chicanos."

"Maybe. You said Chavez was the best mechanic you *had.* Did he quit?"

Orlando nodded.

"What's he doing now?"

"Working as a parking attendant at some fancy restaurant. I don't know the name of the place. He drops in here from time to time to yack with the kids in the garage."

"And now," I asked, "what do you want from me?"

Orlando smiled again, his con man smile this time, for which he had been sent to prison on his first offense. "Well," he began, "I happen to know this famous Ram now enshrined in the Hall of Fame at Canton and I thought he could use his influence to get Kranski to cool it."

"I doubt it. If the kid isn't working for you any more, what's your interest in him?"

The smile faded and he looked at me dolefully. "You couldn't mean that! He's a kid, a kid with a future. Jesus, that was a rotten thing to say!"

"It was," I admitted. "I'll talk to the man."

His smile was back. "I knew you would. You're all heart, Brock!"

"Drop dead," I said.

Karl (Crazy) Kranski; his teammates had nicknamed him Kraz. From my limited knowledge of him on the playing field, I had to assume he would be a hard man to cajole.

I climbed into my ancient Mustang, kept in top condition by the boys in the auto shop at the club. They owed me; I had been the one who had suggested the shop. But they were the ones who had suggested the free repair work (except for parts). Owing and being owed—Orlando had taught them that.

The office of Sergeant Karl Kranski, according to the sign on the door, was shared with a sergeant named Ethel Wingram. It was a small office and Kranski was alone in the room when I entered.

He seemed to be a few pounds heavier than he had been in his playing days. He had weighed in around two hundred and eighty pounds then.

"Remember me?" I asked him.

"I sure as hell do," he said, "and not kindly. What's on your mind, Callahan?"

"A young man named Peter Chavez."

"That Spik punk? Is he a friend of yours?"

"Kraz," I said, "let's make a deal. You don't use the word Spik and I won't call you a Polack."

"That's what I am. And I'm not ashamed of it."

I stared at him. I sighed. I shook my head.

He smiled. "Sit down, you Mick bastard, and tell me why you're here. Do you live in town?"

I nodded and sat on a chair near his desk. "I do. And I was one of the founders of the Tomorrow Club. And Orlando told me this morning you have been even more nasty than your usual self with young Peter Chavez. He asked me to use my NFC influence to get you to lighten up on the lad. If you remember, Orlando was in the AFC."

"I remember. He was also in the can a couple of times. Did he mention that?"

"He didn't have to. I knew it."

"Did he tell you that Chavez no longer works at the Tomorrow Club—and right now might be working for a hoodlum named Chris Andropolus?"

"He told me the first part but not the *might* part. Are you *sure* he's working for this hoodlum? Orlando said he was working as a parking lot attendant at some fancy restaurant in town."

"He was. At the Le Bon Appetit. But not any more. As for his working with Andropolus, I'm sure enough to keep investigating it. And I can't find Chavez to ask him. Does Orlando have his current address?"

"I don't know. You'd have to ask him."

"I will." He smiled again. "I understand old Homer Gallup left you all his money."

"Half of it. Did you know Homer?"

"Sure did. Great guy. A Cowboy fan and a real swinger. We went on a couple of binges together. He used to come from L.A. on the weekends for the games. In his *own* plane! A lot of class to that guy."

As much as I loved Homer, I had never thought of him as classy. Probably to Kranski, class was his euphemism for money.

I stood up. "Well, I have done what Orlando asked me to do and now I will let you get back to your paper work."

"What's your hurry? It's almost time for lunch—on me."

"I'd like that," I lied, "but I'm due in Ventura in half an hour. Some other time maybe."

"Sure. I'll call you."

"Do that," I said. *Some time in the next century*, I thought.

I drove over to Kay Decor from there. Jan was talking with a client when I entered. I sat with Audrey Kay, her boss, and drank strong, thick coffee out of small, thin cups and talked about our Dodgers, who, in the middle of June, were already seven and a half games behind the leader in their division.

Refined and genteel Audrey used some words I'd rather not record about our formerly esteemed heroes, and then the customer left.

"I came to take you to lunch," I told Jan.

"How nice! Where? Not Harry's Chop House?"

"Don't be vulgar. I was thinking of Le Bon Appetit."

She looked at me suspiciously.

"I'll go along," Audrey said. "Blanche can watch the shop. She's a brown bagger."

Blanche was their drudge and could not afford to buy her lunches yet.

We took Jan's Mercedes; my old clunker would look gauche on the Le Bon Appetit parking lot, they decided. What those two know about cars would fit comfortably in a gnat's eye.

I'm not sure what we ate; Jan ordered for me in her new night school adult education San Valdesto City College French.

It wasn't bad, though I thought the sauce tasted better than the meat it was supposed to enhance.

They turned to shop talk over our coffee. I excused myself and went to the bar and ordered a beaker of draft Einlicher, the restaurant's major claim to fame.

Gus, the bartender, looked at me dolefully. "Those goddamned Dodgers!" he said.

"I'd rather not talk about them," I said. "Tell me, do you have an address for a young man who used to work here? His name is Peter Chavez."

He shook his head. "But he might still be living with

his girl friend. She's a waitress here but she only works nights."

"Do you know her address?"

He shook his head again. "The boss does, but he's not here. They lived in her apartment and I know it was somewhere on Alvaro Street. How many Felderstadts can there be on Alvaro Street?" He reached under the counter and brought out a phone book.

There was only one—747 Alvaro Street.

"A real bright and beautiful girl," he told me. "I always thought Pete was an okay guy, too. Now, I heard, he's out for the big buck. That's why he quit here. Man, there wasn't a garage in town that could keep my Datsun perking like Pete did."

I nodded. "The head man at the Tomorrow Club rated him tops. But there are still some sharp boys working there. Try them."

"I will. Tell me, Mr. Callahan, what in hell is wrong with the young people these days? They're all out after the fast and dirty buck."

"It's probably contagious," I said. "They caught it from us."

I had a pleasant surprise waiting for me in the restaurant; Audrey had picked up the tab.

"I invited myself," she explained, "and I can always call it a business expense. What do those IRS people know?"

I could have explained to her in intimate and sordid detail what those IRS people knew about every taxpayer in America above the poverty line. But it would have cost me a sixty dollar lunch. I smiled and thanked her.

She and Jan continued with their shop talk on the way back to the shop. I thought of phoning Orlando from there to learn if he had Peter's current address.

But Gus had described his girl friend as a bright and

beautiful girl. And though I am a faithful husband, I do love to look at bright and beautiful girls.

I climbed into my scorned steed and headed for 747 Alvaro Street.

2

747 ALVARO STREET was an eight unit, one-story apartment building of fieldstone, redwood trim, and brown stucco. It was on a corner lot, four units facing each street. They formed an el, which shielded the swimming pool area in the rear from the prevailing wind.

The mailboxes were in a shake-roofed shelter over the front gate. S. Felderstadt had apartment number five.

There was no answer to my ring. I heard voices coming from the pool area. Through the archway, I could see a pair of middle-aged women in terry cloth robes playing gin rummy at the shaded end of the pool.

At the far end, a short, slim, dark-haired girl and a tall young man with a dark bronze tan and sun-bleached long hair were stretched out on a pair of chaise longues.

I told one of the card players, "I'm looking for a woman named Sarah Felderstadt. I wonder if you could—"

She didn't wait for me to finish. She pointed at the girl on the chaise longue, laid down her cards, and said "Gin!"

"Damn you!" her companion said.

I walked to the other end. Sarah Felderstadt was wearing a minimum bikini; I kept my gaze rigidly on her face as I approached. The man was asleep, dark sunglasses shading his eyes.

"Ms. Felderstadt?" I asked.

She nodded.

I pointed at the man. "Is that Peter Chavez?"

"Not even close," she said. "I wish he was. Are you a police officer? Is that why you're looking for Peter?"

"No. My name is Brock Callahan. I'm doing a favor for a friend, a man named Orlando Davis. Do you know him?"

"Not personally. Peter used to talk about him." She pointed at a vacant chaise longue. "Sit down, Mr. Callahan, and tell me why you're looking for Peter."

Her sleeping partner began to snore softly.

I sat down. "A police officer I know told me that he thought Peter might be involved with a local hoodlum and Orlando's worried about him. Do you know where he is?"

"I don't. Was the police officer named Sergeant Kranski?"

"Yes."

"And is the hoodlum Chris Andropolus?"

"Yes. Do you know him?"

"Only by sight. He comes into the restaurant quite often. I've seen you there, too. I suppose you got my name there. Sergeant Kranski has also questioned me about the connection, but I have no idea if it's true and I told him that."

"And you couldn't even make an educated guess where Peter might be now?"

She shook her head. A gurgling sound replaced the snore of the sleeper.

"Don't mind my friend," she said. "He hibernates when he's not on a surf board. You'd think with a body like that he'd at least be good in bed, wouldn't you?"

"I don't know. I never slept with a surfer."

She laughed. And then she looked sadly out at the pool. "You know, the way Peter kept talking about the big money, I have this feeling he wasn't planning on being too particular about the way he got it. He's a bitter boy. His father deserted the family when he was only eight and his mother left town about a month ago. He has an eleven year old brother he has been trying to support but you can't do that on what Le Bon Appetit pays its parking lot attendants. The boy is in a foundling home—St. Mary's—and Peter is determined to get him out of there."

"He could be a bitter boy but that sounds like he is also a pretty solid young man."

"He is—but God knows where he's heading, chasing the big buck."

"We Anglos call it being upwardly mobile," I said.

She shrugged. "I guess. So Peter leaves and I wind up with that!" She looked at the sleeper.

I laughed.

She smiled. "That thing has wheels, but I'm not sure I'm strong enough. Would you help?" She pointed to the pool.

"I am your humble servant."

We gave it a good running start, enough momentum to send the chair and the sleeper well out into the deep water. From the gin rummy players at the other end came the sound of clapping and the cry of "Bravo!"

I thanked them on the way out for their show of approval.

"He is such a big hunk of nothing!" the laydown player complained. "Sarah deserves so much better. Before he came on the scene, there was this sweetest Mexican boy—"

"Keep the faith," I told them. "I think she is about ready to dump the bum."

Orlando had told me that Chavez dropped in to yack

with the boys from time to time. When, I wondered, had been the last time? I drove to the Tomorrow Club next.

Orlando was in his office but not alone. A thin, olive-skinned youth of about eleven was sitting rigidly in a chair near the doorway. He looked unhappy.

Orlando said, "Meet Pete's brother, Brock. This is Juan Chavez."

"Hi!" I said.

He looked me over coldly, head to toes, and nodded.

Orlando sighed. "He came here looking for his brother."

"And where's his brother?"

"I wish to hell I knew. He hasn't been around for two weeks."

"He no longer works at Le Bon Appetit," I told him. "And his former girl friend doesn't know where he is."

He frowned. "How did you learn all that?"

I told him how I had learned all that, starting with Kranski.

He stared at me. "Man, you have been working, haven't you?"

"It wasn't all work. I had a free lunch at Le Bon Appetit and a poolside conversation with a luscious brunette."

"Is her name Sarah?" Juan asked.

"Yes. Do you know her?"

He nodded. "She came to see me. She told me she and Pete were going to get married and get me out of the Shelter. She's nice."

"She sure is." I looked at Orlando. "That would be the St. Mary's Shelter?"

He nodded. "Juan ran away from there this morning. I phoned Father Murphy and he's coming over to pick him up."

"That's no place for a kid, Orlando. I've seen it. Juan can come home with me."

Orlando said, "Are you crazy?"

And Juan said, "No more gringo foster homes for me!"

"Not even one with a pool?" I asked him. "One where you can have your own room in your own building and good Irish cooking?"

He looked doubtful.

Orlando said, "And what am I supposed to tell Father Murphy?"

"My intermediary, Mrs. Casey, will explain it all to Father Murphy. I am sure he will listen to her or have reason to regret it."

Orlando looked at Juan and so did I.

"Okay," he said. "What can I lose?"

A smart-ass kid, my favorite kind.

We went out. About twenty feet from my car, he asked, "Is that a sixty-five Mustang?"

"A nineteen sixty-six Mustang," I informed him.

"The sixty-fives were the hot ones," he said.

"Juan," I explained patiently, "you are talking of stock models. There is no Mustang in the world as hot as this one. And when your brother shows up, he'll confirm that. Get in!"

When he shows up," he said scornfully. "*If* he shows up."

"Get in," I repeated.

His father had deserted him and then his mother. And now his brother? We rode in silence, except for the impressive rumble of my steed's tailpipes.

"When we turned into the Montevista exit from the freeway, he said, "You're rich, huh?"

"Not as rich as most of the people who live here, but rich enough for me."

"Pete told me he was going to be rich, too."

"It could happen."

"You Irish?"

"One hundred percent."

"They're kind of like Mexicans, aren't they?"

"Kind of. They're more like Mexicans than the English are. But you are an American now and so am I."

He said nothing.

Mrs. Casey, our housekeeper, was out in the front yard, trimming her rose bushes. "And who is this?" she asked.

"This is Juan Chavez," I told her, "a former resident of St. Mary's Shelter. He will be spending some time with us. I'm sure that Father Murphy will be here to complain about that before the sun goes down."

"I look forward to the meeting," she said. "I have been meaning to tell Father Murphy what I think about his Shelter for a long time. Are you hungry, Juan?"

He shrugged. "I could eat, I guess."

"Go and wash up," she said, "and I'll fix you something."

He looked doubtfully at her and then at me.

"This way," I told him. "Your bathroom hasn't been used lately. You can use mine."

"*His* bathroom?" Mrs. Casey asked.

I nodded. "I thought we could clean up the old chauffeur's quarters over the garage for him."

"We?"

"I'll do it, if you insist. This way, Juan."

I led him to my bathroom and then went out and up the dusty steps in the garage to the former chauffeur's quarters. Two minutes later I came down the dusty steps and went into the den and phoned Dave's Dustbusters, a cleaning agency.

I told Dave that if he could get his crew over to the

house in the next hour there would be an extra fifty dollars in it for him.

He assured me they would be there as fast as the traffic would permit.

I went to the bedroom and took off my clothes and put on my trunks and went out to the pool. I was on my twelfth lap when Juan came out to watch me.

I figured twelve laps was enough for now. I climbed out and sat on the edge and asked, "Did she feed you her famous Irish stew?"

He shook his head. "Enchiladas and beans and rice. She's sure bossy!"

I agreed with a nod. "Can you swim?"

"I could if I wanted to," he said. "I never wanted to."

"Do you have underpants on?" I asked.

"Of course!"

"Take off everything but those," I said, "and I'll teach you how to swim. We'll use the shallow end and start with the dog paddle."

He shook his head.

"If you don't," I said firmly, "I'll get dressed and take you back to the Shelter. I don't want *anybody* near this pool who can't swim."

He took off his clothes, all but his Jockey shorts.

I kept him in the shallow end, dog paddling, and he got the hang of it quickly. He hadn't lied; he could swim if he wanted to. Back and forth he paddled across the width of the shallow end.

And then, about an hour later, he turned and paddled out toward the deep end.

"Stop!" I shouted at him. "The water is over your head out there!"

"I know," he called back, and kept on paddling.

A smart-ass gutty kid. . . . Don't dream, I told myself; don't let your sentiment affect your sanity.

"Tomorrow," I told him, "we'll work on the overhand strokes. Dog paddling is for babies."

"Why not now?" he asked.

"All right. But first a little lecture. I don't want you to get the wrong idea about gringos. I'm one and my wife is one and so is Mrs. Casey. And we are not the enemy."

"I know," he said. "But not Orlando, right? He's a nigger."

"No. He is a black man. Are you a Spik?"

"A couple guys called me that. What does it mean?"

"It's a word that creepy people use when they talk about Mexicans and other Spanish-speaking people. And nigger is the word that creeps use for blacks."

"How about Chicano?"

"That is acceptable."

"Okay, Irish," he said. "Let's work on the overhand."

Half an hour later he swam the length of the pool overhand and dog paddled all the way back. There had been a lot of splashing on the trip and a lot of misspent energy. He stood there, breathing heavily, looking up at me for acclamation.

"You are a very fast learner," I told him. "You deserve a dish of ice cream and so do I."

When we went into the house, I said to Mrs. Casey, "I'm surprised that Father Murphy isn't here by now."

"I phoned him," she explained. "He is sending somebody over with Juan's clothing."

"Good work," I said. "Juan and I were wondering if we could have some ice cream."

"Are you going to swim any more?"

We shook our heads.

"Then you can have some," she decreed. "Go sit in the shade and I'll bring it."

We went out into the shade of the overhang. There Juan asked, "Is she the boss here?"

"At times. She and I and my wife take turns being boss."

"Are they going to help you look for my brother?"

I shook my head. "I'm not even sure that I will."

"I wish you would," he said.

"I probably will," I told him.

3

DAVE AND HIS dauntless crew were finished before Jan came home. They had done a fine job on the garage room and I told him so.

"We always do," he said. "About that extra fifty dollars you mentioned, Mr. Callahan, could you make that in cash?"

"Of course. The IRS, huh?"

He shook his head. "Nah. But my wife keeps the books for the firm and—well, there's this horse running at Hollywood Park tomorrow who is a dead cinch to win and—"

"I understand," I said. I could also understand why his wife kept the books.

They left and I took Juan up to show him his new, if temporary, home. His eyes brightened but his voice was as expected. "It's okay," he said.

"It's more than okay and you know it. And you had better keep it neat or you'll answer to Mrs. Casey."

"She doesn't scare me," he said. "*Nobody* scares me."

"Then you're a lot dumber than I thought you were," I told him. "Think of it this way—it's either this or back to the Shelter."

He nodded. "I know. That's why I'm going to keep it clean."

A fearless, smart-ass realist, Juan Chavez.

Jan was home and had already been briefed by Mrs.

Casey when we went back to the house. I had the feeling, polite as she was to the lad, that she had some reservations about what I had done.

Mrs. Casey had catered to Juan's ethnic tastes at lunch, but dinner was all gringo: roast lamb and petit peas and browned new potatoes.

Juan went up to Mrs. Casey's room with her after dinner to watch an old John Wayne movie on the tube. Jan and I sat in the den, watching the MacNeil/Lehrer News Hour.

"You went to a lot of trouble," she said. "He could have slept in my sewing room."

"I suppose. But we need a guest room, don't we? And we can't be sure how long he'll have to stay here."

"Like forever?" she asked.

"Don't be silly!"

A silence, and then she said, "You know, Mr. Macho Man, if your chauvinistic false pride hadn't got in the way, we could have been married twelve years ago. We could have a couple of kids by now."

"Guilty," I agreed. "If you insist, I'll try to find him a foster home among his own people."

"Are you accusing me of racism?"

"No. I was thinking maybe Juan would be happier. And as for the forever bit you mentioned, remember that he has a brother who plans to make a home for him."

"Father Murphy told Mrs. Casey that his brother deserted him."

"It is my personal opinion," I told her, "that Father Murphy doesn't know his ass from third base and I am sure that Mrs. Casey would agree with me."

She sighed. We sat in silence, domestic silence, the worst kind.

About ten minutes later she sighed again. "I guess I've been out-voted, two to one. You win, lover."

"I adore you," I said.

June is usually our overcast month, cool and windless. It was windless tonight but the sky was clear, the moon full, the stars bright.

I lay awake and thought about kids, today's kids, kids on drugs and on the run, fifteen-year-old prostitutes and teenage killers.

And the reading levels kept going down in schools all across the country and the parents complained. The parents watched *Dallas* and the other top rated idiocies on the boob tube, but complained about illiteracy. What was *their* excuse?

"Stop mumbling," Jan said.

The overcast had sneaked in from the ocean during the night. The front lawn was heavy with dew in the morning, including dog dew. The local law decreed that all dogs must be either leashed or kept in a fenced yard. Dog lovers are not always people lovers.

I went over to wake up Juan for breakfast but he was already in the pool, jumping in at the deep end and swimming (overhand) to the far end.

"After breakfast," I told him, "I'll teach you how to dive."

"Mrs. Casey promised me last night that she'd teach me," he said. "We're going to the library and get a book on it."

"Suit yourself," I said stiffly. "Breakfast in fifteen minutes."

Mrs. Casey, spoilsport . . .

Jan is the kitchen boss at breakfast; Mrs. Casey, a late night old-movie addict, doesn't rise that early.

There wasn't much dialogue during the meal. Juan

probably sensed that Jan hadn't fully accepted him yet. Jan could have been feeling guilty about that. I was still resenting Mrs. Casey's intrusion into my domain.

Jan had gone to work and Juan was in his room, making his bed, when Orlando phoned. He told me, "One of our boys was at the drag race in Santa Maria on Sunday. He saw Pete Chavez up there. I'm not sure you should tell Juan that, though."

"Why not?"

"That should mean Pete's still in town. So why hasn't he seen his brother?"

"Maybe he's living in Santa Maria."

"I doubt it. Well, you decide about telling Juan. How is he doing?"

"Better than I expected. He's a sharp kid."

"So is Pete. But if he's tied up with Andropolus, as Kranski claims, sharp isn't enough to keep him out of the slammer. Not that I put much faith in what Kranski says."

"I plan to check it out."

"I'm glad," he said. "Good hunting, brother."

I decided not to tell Juan what Orlando had told me. If his brother was still in town, he had either deserted Juan or possibly decided that the company he was now keeping would not be the proper company for an eleven-year-old boy. I almost hoped it was the latter.

I phoned my good friend Lieutenant Bernard Vogel to learn if he would be in his office that day.

"For the morning," he told me. "I'll be in court this afternoon. What's on your mind?"

"A young man named Peter Chavez and a hoodlum named Chris Andropolus."

He chuckled. "I saw you come out of Kranski's office yesterday. Now I know why. Look, I'll be busy until ten-thirty. I'll talk with you after that."

"I'll be there," I promised.

Why had he chuckled? What was funny? It was probable that Bernie would have even more contempt for Kranski than Orlando had. Bernie was the intellectual type.

The sun was starting to break through the overcast when I drove down to the station. Bernie was in with the chief, the desk sergeant told me; I waited in his office.

There was no hint of nicotine in the air; that meant five months of non-addiction for a former three-pack-a-day smoker. He should be over the hump by now.

I complimented him on that when he came in.

"I still dream about the damned things," he said. "And Ellie claims I'm hard to live with."

Ellie is his wife. "You were always hard to live with," I said. "What's so funny about Kranski's concern with Pete Chavez?"

"Because it's not Pete he's after," he explained. "It's Andropolus. He's like a man on a crusade about him."

"Why Andropolus? He's not a juvenile."

"That's for sure. But he's married to Kranski's niece. And though Kranski claims the girl is a tramp, I suspect she was once his pride and joy. He has no kid of his own, you know."

"I didn't. This Andropolus, from what I read in the papers, is our new vice king in town, right?"

"Right. Often indicted, never convicted. He came up here about a year ago. The word I get from down south, the big boys ran him out of L.A. He tried Phoenix after that but those Italians run a tight family and it doesn't include Greeks."

"How about Chief Harris? Doesn't he feel that Kranski is getting involved in a field outside his jurisdiction?"

Bernie smiled. "If he does, he hasn't mentioned it.

You have to remember that the chief has a socially ambitious wife, and Kranski is married to a Woolrick. That would be the Woolrick Department Store people, big money and old money, going back to revolutionary days."

"Oh, boy! But kids? What kind of organization can Andropolus hope to make out of them?"

"You'd have to ask him that. They're streetwise kids, mostly Chicanos. It's this lower Main Street end of town he hopes to take over. They've had their gangs here for years, though there's been a truce lately. So maybe he can con them into believing they can move up into the majors with him, into the big money."

"He's going to have to butt heads with some hot-headed papas who run their own penny ante scams."

Bernie nodded. "I'm sure he's learned that in the last year and hired the local help he needs or brought them along from Los Angeles." He paused. "And now tell me why you're interested in all this."

I told him the whole story, from Orlando's request to Juan's moving in with us.

His smile was cynical. "You keep an eye on the kid. Count the silverware every day."

I shook my head. "Not this kid, not Juan."

"Count the silverware," he repeated. "I don't want that ham-handed Kranski stirring up any new trouble down here. It's not only the kids who resent us in this part of town. You said it yourself, there are a lot of hotheaded papas—and many of them carry knives."

"I would too if I lived down here."

"So would I," he admitted. "Keep in touch, footballer."

"I'll keep in touch," I promised. "And I expect the same courtesy from you."

"What does that mean?"

"It means that I, a still bonded and licensed private

investigator, have been hired by the Tomorrow Club to find Peter Chavez. Naturally, I will expect full police cooperation on this."

"Dear God!" he said. "Here we go again!"

"Of course," I continued, "I could talk with Chief Chandler Harris and suggest I work with Kranski."

"You win," he said wearily.

"Gracias, amigo," I said. *"Adios."*

"Go!" he said.

I went. I went to Rubio's Rendezvous, a narrow bar wedged between a deserted pawn shop and an active massage parlor off lower Main Street. Rubio's wines and hard liquor were not exactly vintage, but his Mexican beer was.

As a sideline, Rubio pooled the minuscule bets of his horse and sports gamblers and laid them off to a kinsman who would have rejected them individually. For which, of course, Rubio charged a small commission.

There were only three patrons in the place. They were sitting at a corner table, sipping red wine and playing some three-handed card game I couldn't understand.

"Pancho!" he greeted me. "It's been a long time. Trouble again?"

I shook my head. "I came for information and a small beer. I came to ask about a man named Chris Andropolus."

"He's trouble," Rubio said, "but nothing we can't handle."

"You know the man?"

"I've never met him." He poured my beer and took a card from a drawer in the back bar. "This is the man he sent."

Tony Toledo, the card read. There was a phone number, but no address. It was a name I dimly remembered from my Los Angeles days but I couldn't place it at the moment.

"What did he want?" I asked.

"He said he could lay off my big bets. I told him I had no big bets. He told me he could get any drug I wanted. I told him I did not deal in drugs. He told me he'd be back." Rubio paused. "Nothing personal, Pancho, but I also told him this was not gringo country."

"There are plenty of gringos in this neighborhood, Rubio."

He smiled. "But here they are the minority. Like we are where you live."

"Ouch!" I said.

"No offense," he said. "You are our honorary Chicano."

"Thank you. Do you know a young man named Peter Chavez?"

"I know several of that name but they are not young. Pancho, don't worry about this Andropolus. We will take care of him. He is not the first who has tried to move in here."

"Don't you think it would be wiser to let the police take care of him?"

He made a face. "You know better than that. They don't give a damn about us! They're not like you."

I didn't argue with him. I laid a bill on the bar and said, "Please be careful."

He nodded, and pushed the bill back at me. "On the house. Go with God, amigo."

It was now close to noon. I went home for lunch. Mrs. Casey was in the kitchen. Juan was sitting at the shaded end of the pool, wearing bright blue swimming trunks and a sad countenance.

"They didn't have any books on diving at the library," he said glumly.

"I'll teach you. New trunks?"

He nodded. “Mrs. Casey bought them for me. She’s nice, isn’t she?”

“Quite often,” I admitted. “But we had better try some practice dives before lunch. Mrs. Casey has this old-fashioned idea that a swimmer can get cramps if he tries to swim right after lunch.”

“That’s okay,” he said. “We got some other books at the library.”

He held them up for me to see. *Thunder Road* was one title, *Speedway Challenge* another. The third was *Dirt Track Summer.*

“How come no football books?” I asked.

He shook his head. “Cars, that’s what I like. And Pete, too.”

We got in some practice dives before Mrs. Casey called us to lunch. He couldn’t quite get the knack of using the spring in his legs to reach out for a shallow dive; they were all belly-floppers. But I knew he would manage eventually. Because he wanted to.

Mrs. Casey went up to her daytime dramas after lunch. Juan sat in the shade of the overhang and started *Thunder Road.* I went into the den for a brief hibernation.

I was halfway into dreamland when I remembered where I had seen the name of Tony Toledo. It had been in the *Times.* He had been a minor hoodlum in Los Angeles who had put a Hollywood stunt man in the hospital for allegedly messing around with Tony’s wife. Before his hoodlum period, he had been a fair to middling club fighter.

Rubio could be right; Toledo was no threat. But it was highly likely that Andropolus had brought along some soldiers from smogtown who might be more menacing. There were enough of them down there.

4

JUAN WAS STILL reading when I came out for our lesson. He put the book down and asked, "When are you going to start looking for Pete?"

"I asked around downtown about him this morning," I said.

"Nothing?"

I considered telling him what Orlando had told me but decided not to. Attending a drag race didn't seem to be excuse enough for deserting a brother. "Nothing," I said.

"I know who his best friend is," he told me. "Maybe you could ask him."

"So could you. Do you know his phone number?"

He shook his head. "I don't think he has a number of his own. Pete told me he lives in a rooming house. But I know where he works. He works nights at that Union gas station on the corner of Guerero and Cortez. His name is Fernando Schultz." He frowned. "I guess his father is a German."

"I'll go there tonight," I promised. "Come on, it's time for your lesson."

"Couldn't I finish this book first?" he asked. "It's real exciting."

"Holler when you're ready," I said.

I went into the house and looked up the telephone number of the Union Oil station on Guerero and Cortez.

A woman answered and I asked if Fernando Schultz was still working there and at what hours.

"Is he in trouble?" she asked.

"Not that I know of. I'm calling from the Tomorrow Club and we're trying to locate a friend of his."

Fernando, she told me, worked the shift from eight o'clock to four in the morning. The boy must be hungry; that was a dangerous time for a station to be open in that neighborhood. But it was close to the freeway and they probably picked up trade from the night travelers.

And then, as long as the book was open, I looked up the listing for Tony Toledo. There was none. I phoned the number on the card that Rubio had given me. There was no answer.

Juan was still reading. I pulled a book of Cheever short stories from the shelf in the den and went out to take the chair next to his.

An hour later, he said, "I'm finished."

"Give me five more minutes," I said. "You're a fast reader."

"The fastest in my class," he said.

"What grade are you in?"

"I was in seventh grade. I'll be in eighth next semester. But I'll be twelve then. My birthday is in August."

"Where do you go to school?"

"At Saint Benedict's."

Some kids read; the sisters make damned sure of that.

Three minutes later he was back in the pool. Two hours after that he could dive better than I could. Of course, he was a lot skinnier. It's easy for skinny guys.

We were having ice cream again when he asked, "Could I go along with you tonight when you talk to Fernando?"

I shook my head. "His shift doesn't start until ten o'clock. You'll be in bed by then."

He smiled. "I'll be in my room. How do you know if I'll be in bed?"

"Because I trust you."

He said nothing.

I had lied to him twice in the last couple hours, first about learning nothing today and now about the time of my trip. My deserted but still dormant Catholicism stirred uneasily. I almost convinced myself it was for his own good.

He picked up my empty dish and the spoon and took them with him to the kitchen. I went back to Cheever. He came out and opened *Speedway Challenge.*

We were still reading when Jan came home.

"What a pleasant domestic scene," she said. "And Brock Callahan reading Cheever! Did you finish all your Tarzan books?"

Juan laughed.

"Don't encourage her," I told him. "She can get worse."

She leaned over and kissed me. "A martini?"

"A double. And a Coke for Juan."

"Yes, master," she said, and went back into the house.

"She's sure pretty," Juan said.

"That she is."

"She's almost as pretty as Sarah Felderstadt. I wish Pete would have stayed with her. We'd all be together now."

"Maybe some time in the future you will all be together," I said, my third lie of the day.

"Maybe," he agreed, but there was no conviction in his voice.

It was John Wayne week on Mrs. Casey's favorite station. Juan went up to watch with her after dinner. Jan took the samples she had brought home and laid them out on the dining room table, seeking the perfect match for drapes, upholstery, and carpeting.

I took a chance that Juan wouldn't be down again early enough to learn I had left well before ten o'clock. I took the freeway to the Cortez Street exit and drove the short block to Guerero Street.

A big semi was on the drive, loading up with diesel fuel. I parked on the street and went into the station. The young man servicing the semi was black; it didn't seem likely that his name was Fernando Schultz.

The young man plugging a nail hole in a tire in the station looked more German than Spanish. He was a fairly tall and stocky youth with short blond hair, a square jaw, and light blue eyes.

"Mr. Schultz?" I asked him.

He nodded.

"I work with the Tomorrow Club," I said, "and—"

"I know you do," he interrupted. "I've seen you there. You're Brock Callahan, aren't you?"

"Yes. Juan Chavez told me you are his brother's best friend."

He shook his head. "Not any more."

"Do you know where he is now?"

He shook his head again. "Pete's deserted his old friends. And his brother, too, the way I heard it. The kid's still in Saint Mary's Shelter."

"Not any more," I said. "He's staying with us. I have a feeling that wanting to get Juan out of the Shelter is the reason Pete has got himself involved with some hairy characters."

"Maybe," he said, "and maybe not. When he was working at that restaurant he was living with a waitress who worked there. Between the two of them they earned enough to keep Juan with them. But then he suddenly dumps her. She went to visit Juan more than Pete did."

"Sarah Felderstadt?" I asked.

"That's the girl. A real looker, and nice, too." He took a breath. "You know, there was always a lot of loner in Pete. And a heavy urge for the big buck. But he ain't got the smarts Juan has. He's a cinch to wind up in the can—or in his grave. I heard he's got himself tied up with some Greek from L.A. who's trying to take over this end of town."

I nodded. "Chris Andropolus."

"Whatever." He smiled and shook his head. "Wait until that Greek runs into the San Valdesto Brotherhood. He'll wish to hell he never saw this town."

"Let's hope so," I said. "Thanks, Fernando."

"Any time," he said.

The San Valdesto Brotherhood (and the town) had been named after a saint who was no longer recognized in Rome but still revered by the local Chicanos. According to Rubio, one of the founders, its members had been gang ruffians themselves in their younger days. Today they were determined that their kids would not follow the same pattern. They were not always successful.

The light was on in the room over the garage when I pulled into our driveway.

Jan was in the dining room, still pondering samples. Juan, she told me, had become bored with John Wayne and gone to his room to read.

"A smart move," I said. "I hope he didn't notice I had left the house."

"I don't think he did. Why?"

"I told him I wasn't going over to see his brother's friend until ten o'clock."

"You shouldn't lie to children. Did you learn anything?"

"I learned that Juan might be with us for a while."

"That's fine with me," she said. "Do you know what

he told Mrs. Casey? He told her I was the prettiest woman he had ever seen."

I smiled.

"What's so funny about that?" she asked.

"Well, Juan and I had this dialogue. And we both agreed that you are almost as pretty as Sarah Felderstadt."

She looked at me suspiciously. "Who's Sarah Felderstadt?"

"A mutual friend of ours. Children shouldn't lie to adults."

"One more time," she said. "Who is Sarah Felderstadt?"

"His brother's former live-in girl friend. She is a waitress at Le Bon Appetit."

She frowned. "A slim, short, dark-haired girl?"

"That's the one."

"For your information, mister roving eye, I was prettier than that when I was her age."

"I am sure you were. Would you like some cocoa?"

She shook her head.

"Yes, you would. Honey, I had to pay you back for that Tarzan shot of yours. I'll put some cinnamon in it and make it with cream."

"Later," she said. "I'm almost finished here."

I went into the den to watch the last part of the John Wayne movie. It was ending when Jan came in with two cups of cocoa. She handed me a cup and switched to the PBS channel. She sat next to me on the couch, friends again.

She said, "Mrs. Casey was wondering why Corey hasn't been around lately."

Corey Raleigh was my protégé, a young man I had trained for our tawdry trade. I told her, "He's in the army reserve and he's spending his obligatory three weeks on maneuvers at Fort Leslie."

Jan sighed. "Poor Mrs. Casey, a natural mother married to a sterile husband. Well, she has Juan now. That should keep her happy for a while."

"She never told *me* her husband was sterile."

"It is not a subject that Mrs. Casey would even think of discussing with a man."

We watched "Fawlty Towers" on PBS, a double showing tonight, and then switched to a commercial channel for the eleven o'clock news. It was more commercial than it was news; Jan turned it off and we went to bed.

I couldn't get to sleep. Apparently neither could Jan. Finally she said, "If we can't sleep, let's put our time to better use.

Which we did.

5

JAN WENT TO WORK early next morning; Saturday was a big day at Kay Decor. The out-of-town customers came for a festive weekend at our hotels along the ocean. Mrs. Casey and Juan rode downtown with Jan. Mrs. Casey had decided Juan needed a replenishment of his sparse and well-worn wardrobe.

I was running out of people to ask about the whereabouts of Peter Chavez. It was time to go directly to the horse's mouth. I looked up the address of Christopher Andropolus in the phone book.

It wasn't far from where we live, though in a more expensive section of Montevista. I tried to think of some neighborly opening as I drove there. I discarded the idea of identifying myself as a courier for the welcome wagon. The truthful approach was the best; I was trying to locate a possible employee of his.

The Andropolus place was a low but large home of lannon stone and brown stucco with a heavy cedar shake roof. It was at the peak of the rise and commanded a 360-degree view of the Santa Ynez Valley behind it and the ocean and the town below from the front.

There was a BMW on the driveway and a Clenet convertible visible through the open garage door. The Clenet was a locally built custom car that had suffered the same fate as Mr. DeLorean's famous fiasco.

A slim blonde wearing designer jeans, a light blue

turtleneck sweater, and a badly discolored right eye opened the door to my ring.

"Mrs. Andropolus?" I asked.

She nodded.

"My name is Brock Callahan. Is your husband home?"

She nodded again. "Are you selling something?"

I shook my head. "I live down the road a ways. I work for a local youth organization. One of our boys moved without telling us and we heard that he might be working for your husband. His brother is worried about him."

"Wait here," she said.

She was back in a few minutes. "Come in."

I followed her down a long hall to the room closest to the living room archway. The door was open. Chris Andropolus was sitting in there behind a teakwood desk, attired in a black satin robe edged with scarlet piping. Mrs. Andropolus closed the door and left.

He stood up as I entered. He was short and wide and bulky. He had an old-fashioned crew cut and a small scar below his right eye.

He asked, "Are you the Brock Callahan who used to play football for the Rams?"

I nodded.

"What's this about a missing boy?" he asked.

"His name is Peter Chavez," I said. "He missed a few meetings at a youth club of which I am a sponsor, and his younger brother told us he had not seen him for weeks. I have been asking around and"—I smiled,—"your name came up."

"From where?"

I shrugged. "The director of the club didn't tell me that."

He smiled back at me. "Footballer, let's play it straight. Sergeant Kranski sent you, didn't he?"

"Sergeant Kranski?"

"Don't look so dumb," he said. "I remember now that you went into detective work after you left the Rams. Don't tell me you don't know Karl Kranski."

"I knew him as an opponent. We were never friends. Is he with the police department here in town?"

"Yes. And he is my wife's uncle. And he is the man who gave her that black eye you might have noticed. Do you want to stick with this phony comedy routine or should we talk sense?"

"Let's talk sense," I said. "Is Peter Chavez working for you?"

He shrugged. "I have no idea. I don't recognize the name. But I have a variety of business interests in town and it's possible he could be one of my employees."

"Would Tony Toledo know if Chavez is one of them?"

"Who is Tony Toledo?" he asked.

"You suggested we talk sense," I reminded him.

He gave that some thought before he said, "You could ask Tony. I'll give you his phone number."

"I already have it. Could you give me his address?"

He shook his head.

"So be it," I said. "And now for a bit of neighborly advice. There are men in this town who could be much more dangerous to your health than your wife's uncle. Quite a few of them carry knives. That is an ugly, painful way to die, Mr. Andropolus."

There was scorn in his smile. "I'll be careful. I'm sure you can find your way out, footballer."

Mrs. Andropolus was pruning a rose bush near the garage when I came out. She beckoned me over.

"Did my uncle send you here?" she asked.

I shook my head.

"You know him, don't you?"

"Yes. Your husband told me he gave you that black eye."

"He did. He's crazy!"

"That's why his teammates called him Kraz," I said. "But I never thought he'd sink low enough to hit a woman."

She sighed. "Neither did I. God, he was closer to me than my father when I was a kid. And now—" She shook her head. "He came here when Chris wasn't home and tried to talk me into leaving him. I told him to get lost, and he backhanded me and stormed out."

I said nothing.

"I suppose," she went on, "that since he married money and moved to this fancy town he's probably ashamed of a niece married to a Greek."

I doubted that, but didn't voice the doubt.

"I hope you find that boy you're looking for," she told me.

I smiled at her. "So does your uncle. And *I* hope you two make up."

"Never!" she said.

What a sweet little innocent. Unless she was dumber than she looked or sounded, she had to suspect that her husband was not your standard American businessman. Even if she didn't suspect it, Kranski certainly must have informed her.

Kranski and I shared one lack; both of us were childless. His niece was probably his Juan. How sharper than a serpent's tooth is a thankless child. . . .

Through the twelve years of our courtship, I had been reasonably faithful to Jan. Kranski had wandered from wench to wench, according to the players I had met who knew him well. I remembered one story his roomie, Jess Washington, had told me after Jess retired from his playing days in Dallas and became defense coordinator for the Rams.

There was a girl named Della Rivera, a dancer in some

Dallas honky-tonk, who had lasted longer than the others with Kranski. They were, according to Jess, only a few steps short of making it legal when Della infected Kranski with a heavy dose of syphilis.

Like all primitive thinkers, Kranski had probably extended that personal experience into a blanket indictment. We all have our individual bigotries. Overpaid quarterbacks was one of mine.

The headquarters of the San Valdesto Brotherhood was about a block from the Tomorrow Club. I drove there next. It was a small, weathered stucco building, a converted store. The door opened directly into the meeting room, a square room furnished with about fifty folding chairs. The small office of Ricardo Cortez, the director, was partitioned off in one corner.

His door was open. Ricardo was sitting behind a chipped, blue-enameled steel desk. He was an enormous man with a full, gray-streaked black beard and bushy bone-white eyebrows.

He smiled at me. "Mr. Callahan! I can guess why you're here. Your friend Rubio told me of your visit to his bar."

"And what did you guess from that?" I asked.

"That you wish to get involved in our . . . our . . ." He shrugged. "Our current problem."

"Is his name Chris Andropolus?"

"Yes. But, as Rubio told you, we are well equipped to handle our problems with him."

"No gringo need apply—is that what you're saying?"

His face stiffened. "Nothing of the kind. You are well respected in this neighborhood, Mr. Callahan."

"Thank you. So far, my only interest is trying to find Peter Chavez for his brother. As for the other, I moved to this town because I like this town, all of it. And I hate hoodlums. My father was killed by a hoodlum. This isn't your town, Mr. Cortez, this is *our* town."

He smiled cynically. "It would be nice if the police thought as you do."

"Some of them do."

"Not enough of them, not since Chief Harris took over. Mr. Callahan, I am not trying to be rude. I am trying to protect you from possible violence." He smiled. "We need you alive and well."

"I need me the same way. If you get any word on Peter Chavez, you'll let me know, won't you?"

"Of course," he said.

From there to the Tomorrow Club. Orlando was in his office, his feet on his desk, a can of beer in his hand.

"A fine example to the kids you are," I told him, "sitting there and swilling beer."

"It's better than the stuff that they were on," he said. "Did you come down to check me out again?"

"I quit that a long time ago and you know it. I have just come from a talk with Ricardo Cortez. He made it clear to me that it wasn't personal, but a Chicano is a Chicano and I wasn't one of them."

"Those old-timers feel the same way about us blacks," he told me, "and some of the young ones have inherited it. You see, Brock, when you whites were importing blacks, Cortez's people were already here. We're both intruders." He reached into the small refrigerator behind him and tossed me a can of beer. "Are you still looking for Pete Chavez?"

I nodded. "And I'm nowhere." I gave him the story of my adventures since my last visit.

He shook his head. "Tell me, in your playing days, when the score was forty-five to zilch against you with a minute to play, did you still go all out?"

"Yup."

"So did I. I guess we're both damned fools."

"It was personal," I explained.

He smiled. "With jocks, it's *always* personal. But we ain't jocks no more, man."

"Speak for yourself," I said. "I have the same waistline I had twenty years ago."

"But a much fatter wallet," he pointed out. "Relax, man; get your enjoys!"

"I will when you do," I told him. "Thanks for the beer. Give me the word if you hear from Chavez."

"Yowza, massa! Carry on!"

Two hundred and seventy pounds of blithe spirit, Orlando Davis . . .

I went to Kay Decor from there to learn if I could buy Jan a less expensive lunch than Audrey had bought us yesterday.

She was having lunch with a client, she told me. "But guess who came in to see me this morning?"

"Robert Redford?"

"Mrs. Karl Kranski, the former Lois Woolrick. She invited us to dinner tonight. And your good friend Chief Harris and his less than charming wife will also be there."

"Oh, God! What did you tell her?"

"Don't shout now, but I said yes. Audrey would cut my heart out with a dull knife if I refused an invitation from a Woolrick."

"I suppose you couldn't go alone?"

She stared at me.

"You win," I said. "Have a nice and profitable lunch."

Trivial chatterbox Angela Harris, unctuous Chandler Harris, red-neck Karl Kranski and (probably) DAR member Lois Woolrick—what a fascinating evening was in store for me! I went home.

Juan and Mrs. Casey weren't back from town yet and

we were still half an hour from lunchtime. If they didn't get back before then, I would make my own.

I phoned Toledo's number again and this time a woman answered. I asked for Tony.

He was not home, she told me. Could he call me back?

"Please," I told her. "My name is Brock Callahan and—"

"Oh, *you!* " she said. "I've called you twice this morning. Tony asked me to phone you and tell you that he does not know anyone named Peter Chavez. Does that make sense to you?"

"Yes."

"I'm glad," she said, "because it didn't make any sense to me. Who is Peter Chavez?"

"He's a Hollywood stunt man who moved up here last week," I told her, and hung up.

Andropolus had obviously phoned Tony after I left his house. He had denied knowing Peter and now Toledo had confirmed it. Either both of them had lied or one—or they were telling the truth. Whatever, that was the last source I had.

Mrs. Casey and Juan came home a few minutes later. The bundles they were loaded down with made me suspect that Mrs. Casey expected that Juan would be here for a long stay. Or maybe only hoped.

Juan's first question to me was, "Did you find Pete? Do you know where he is?"

I shook my head.

"Do you think maybe he's—he's—" he asked, and couldn't finish.

"No," I said.

6

"I THINK," Jan said when she came home, "that Audrey is mistaken if she thinks Mrs. Kranski is interested in redecorating her house."

"Why?"

"Because she told me having us for dinner was her husband's idea. She told me you were a friend of his."

"An opponent," I said. "Never a friend. He played for the Dallas Cowboys."

"Well, maybe she thinks that gives you two a common bond. Anyway, it was Angela Harris who told her you were married to me. And Mrs. Kranski said she had heard of me through some of her friends in Beverly Hills."

"Who were your clients," I pointed out. "Audrey could be right."

"Maybe. Why would a Woolrick marry a—a police sergeant?"

"A lot of refined women marry clods. You did."

She gave that some thought and decided, "That's true." She smiled. "A little joke, master."

"Save your little jokes for the dinner," I advised her. "You are going to be in very dull company."

The house we were heading for, Jan told me on the way, had been one of several homes around the world where the Woolricks resided, depending on the seasons. Lois had grown up in Pasadena where the old money lived in those days. The Montevista place had been their summer home.

"Where did you learn all that?" I asked her.

"From Audrey. She's a San Valdesto native."

In my plebeian view, a summer home meant one of those rough board, informal cottages in the woods or overlooking a lake where the middle class escaped from the urban grind.

This was not one of those. It was a two-story place of white plaster embedded with decorative pierced shells, ornamented with scrolls, its narrow windows fronted with black wrought iron grilles.

"Eeek!" I said.

"Rococo," Jan said.

"What does that mean?"

"Eighteenth century bad taste. I hope this is a social dinner."

The woman who met us at the door was less ornate, a tall and full-bodied woman in a simple blue silk dress and no jewelry except for a pearl necklace and a plain gold wedding ring.

Her face was as plain as her dress, her smile warm. "It was kind of you to come on such short notice," she said. She turned her smile on me. "But you must know how impetuous Karl can be."

"I certainly do," I agreed.

I thought Jan winced when we came into the high-ceilinged living room but it looked okay to me. Good old-fashioned carved furniture and a lot of brown velour—solid, comfortable stuff.

Karl was standing at the far end of the room. "The Rock!" he said. "We finally meet on friendly turf."

I dredged up a smile. "Finally."

"Bourbon?" he asked.

I nodded. "Please. With water."

He shook his head. "Diluting good booze with water! No wonder you Rams were pushovers."

"Karl, for heaven's sake!" Lois said.

I smiled at her. "He was only joking. And he has the lumps to prove it."

That is a sample of the opening dialogue. It got higher as the cocktail hour progressed but not much higher. Roly-poly Chandler Harris and his undernourished chatterbox wife helped to keep it well below the Noel Coward level.

Lois Kranski sat at the far end of the room after dinner. She seemed to be more my kind of people. I went over to sit next to her on the couch.

"Are they boring you?" she asked me.

"A little."

"They're boring me—but Chandler is Karl's superior." She paused. "My niece phoned this afternoon. She told me you paid her husband a visit this morning."

"I did. I am trying to locate a boy who seems to be missing. Perhaps Karl told you about him?"

She shook her head. "Karl tells me very little about his work. But Shirley told me today that he went up to her house and actually struck her. I almost canceled the dinner. What about this boy who is missing?"

"His name is Peter Chavez. He's one of Karl's probationers. He has a younger brother who is boarding with us. *His* name is Juan. Their parents deserted them and now it looks as if Juan's brother has deserted him."

"Is that the boy you mentioned to Shirley?"

"Yes. Karl thinks he's working for Chris Andropolus."

"And Karl doesn't think he should? Why not?"

"The man's a hoodlum!"

"You sound just like Karl," she said. "Has Chris *ever* been convicted of any crime? Never! But because he's married to Karl's only niece, the man's a hoodlum. That is strange thinking for an officer of the law."

"Mrs. Kranski," I said, "the world is full of—"

"Call me Lois," she interrupted.

"Okay. Lois, the world is full of unconvicted criminals. Chris Andropolus has one named Tony Toledo working for him and—"

"I happen to know Tony," she interrupted again, "and why he was in trouble. He assaulted a man who had been involved with his wife. And I am sure that both you and Karl would have done the same."

"We might," I said patiently. "But I'm sure neither of us would traffic in drugs. And that is what Tony Toledo suggested to one of my lower Main Street friends. You can't believe that Chris Andropolus is a legitimate businessman!"

"Yes, I can," she said firmly. "A man is innocent until he is proven guilty. And if what you told me is true about Tony, I'm going to tell Chris about it."

I said nothing.

She put a hand on mine. "Brock, I was sure we were going to get along. I've been a bad hostess."

"You have not," I assured her. "I am used to opposing opinions. Karl and I had opposing opinions every time we met. Should we join the others?"

She shook her head. "Except for Jan, they're too dull. Is it true you are in the football Hall of Fame?"

I nodded. "But I'd rather hear about your ancestors. You come from a long American heritage, don't you?"

She gave it to me, generation by generation. She started with Great Grandfather Ludington Woolrick, who had opened a store in Boston in Colonial days, and went on through the generations that followed. Though her words were laudatory, I somehow got the feeling that several of those pirates were no more honest than Chris Andropolus.

Then Kranski came over to tell her she was neglecting her guests.

"Not this one," she said. She winked at me and went over to join the others.

Kranski sat down next to me. "I understand you've been looking for Pete Chavez."

"I have."

"And Jan just told me his brother is staying with you."

"He is."

"I'd like to talk to him."

"Over my dead body!"

"Don't be a hardhead, Brock. Harris is backing me on this."

"My attorneys will back me. Karl, I've learned more about Peter Chavez the last couple of days than Juan knows. I heard he was up at that drag race in Santa Maria last Sunday and that's the last I've heard. Why this obsession about Peter Chavez?"

"Because we have some leverage with him, including violation of probation. We have no lever we can use on the rest of that crew. Promise me that if you locate Chavez you'll let me know."

"I'll let somebody down there know," I said. "But not a man who gave his own niece a black eye."

"Did Lois tell you about that?"

"Your niece did. I went up there to warn Andropolus that if he tried to organize those lower Main Street bush leaguers he could die before his time."

"Jesus, you were really asking for it, weren't you?"

"Nope. It was a friendly warning. Neither you nor Andropolus have been in this town long enough to know how real mean those Latin types can get when a gringo tries to take over."

He shook his head and expelled a long breath. "Thanks for the Santa Maria tip. Want a drink?"

"We have to be getting home," I told him. "Jan had a hard day. She almost decided she couldn't make it here tonight."

We left ten minutes later.

In the car, Jan said, "You and Lois seemed to be enjoying each other."

"More or less."

"While I sat there being buried in platitudes, non sequiturs, and euphemisms. I hope they don't think we owe them a dinner."

"Tell 'em you're a Democrat," I suggested. "That will cool 'em."

"And put Kay Decor out of business. No, thanks!"

There was no light in the room above the garage, but the glow of her TV set was visible in Mrs. Casey's room when we came home.

"Cocoa?" I asked.

"Not tonight. I'm bushed!"

She went to bed. I stayed up for the eleven o'clock news. I forget now what it was; I didn't pay much attention. I was still remembering the stubborn belief of Lois Woolrick Kranski in the innocence of Chris Andropolus.

New money knows what goes on in the real world; that's how they got there. But old money lives in its own insular world.

At breakfast, Jan said, "We haven't played golf for weeks. Why don't we go out for nine holes this afternoon after the crowd is gone?"

"Let's," I said, and looked at Juan. "Do you want to come along? You can be Jan's caddy."

"I can't," he said. "Mrs. Casey and I are going to late mass and then she's going to take me to the zoo."

Mrs. Casey had failed to convert Corey; she now had a son she didn't have to convert.

The phone rang and Jan answered it. "I can't say I had a good time," she said, "but I tried to pretend I did." A pause. "I didn't get to talk with her much. She spent most of her time talking to Brock." Another pause. "I doubt very much that she plans to do any redecorating. But we can hope."

"Audrey?" I asked, when Jan came back to the table.

She nodded. "She's getting so pushy!"

"That's how the non money gets to be the new money," I explained. "By taking it from the old money."

Juan laughed.

"Don't encourage him," Jan said.

A somnolent Sunday in a San Valdesto suburb. Mrs. Casey and Juan left for church. I watched the Dodgers lose to the Mets in far away New York. Jan read the papers, local and L.A.

Then she and I got in nine holes where she relieved me of four dollars at fifty cents a hole. I managed a tie on the ninth. My beloved bride has the true hustler's handicap.

We were having our drinks before dinner when Orlando phoned. "It's started," he told me.

"What's started?"

"The war," he said. "Somebody just bombed the headquarters of the San Valdesto Brotherhood."

7

THE LOCAL RADIO station, which I tuned in after Orlando's phone call, reported that the bomb had been an incendiary bomb. The damage to the Brotherhood headquarters had been minimal, thanks to the quick response of the city fire department. It was estimated at approximately seven thousand dollars.

Seven thousand dollars could be minimal to radio stations; it seemed reasonable to assume it would not be minimal to the low-income soldiers of the Brotherhood. Orlando was right. The war had started. And though insurance would probably recompense them for the loss, payment in kind was sure to be their answer to the opening attack.

The local news on the tube at six o'clock confirmed that. A brush fire in the dry gulch below the home of Christopher Andropolus had been determined as the work of an arsonist by the county fire department. The damage to the Andropolus home had been estimated at twenty thousand dollars.

The Brotherhood had fought fire with fire and wound up thirteen thousand dollars ahead. The sheriff's department had a suspect they were holding but refused to identify at this time.

Juan had been watching with me. He said, "I started a fire once."

"Did you mean to?" I asked him.

"I'm not sure," he said. "My mother said I did. I told her it was an accident. I guess that was a lie. Pete said that sometimes we have to lie. Do you believe that?"

"No," I lied.

The morning radio gave us further information at breakfast. A suspect in the arson at the Brotherhood office had also been picked up by the city police, and this time the names of both suspected arsonists were revealed. Both were Latino names. Brother against brother and son against father; Andropolus had waved the magic lure of the big buck and induced the young to deny their heritage.

"I know that one guy," Juan said. "He's a friend of Pete's."

"Which one?"

"Chico Ruiz."

Ruiz was being held as a suspect for the Andropolus fire. I said nothing.

"I never liked Chico," Juan said. "I don't know why Pete does. He got Pete that job at the restaurant." He made a face. "Parking cars! Pete's a mechanic!"

"At the Tomorrow Club," I pointed out. "Orlando pays bottom dollar there. Pete probably made more on tips alone when he worked at the restaurant."

"Maybe," Juan admitted. "Then why did Chico quit? He had the job before Pete."

I shrugged. "Let's think of the bright side. That's where Pete met Sarah Felderstadt."

"Sure! And left her. The stupid jerk!"

Again, I said nothing. Jan said, "Another piece of French toast, Juan?"

Jan went to work after breakfast, Juan to his room, and I down to the Tomorrow Club to get the latest battle report from the front. Orlando was in the gym, shooting baskets from the free throw line. I watched him miss four out of five.

"How's Juan behaving?" he asked me.

"Like a little gentleman. I came to find out if you have any information on a young man named Chico Ruiz."

"Let's go to my office," he said, "and I'll tell you over a couple of beers."

"One beer," I said. "I don't drink in the morning."

"Whatever you say, whitey."

The way it was, he told me in his office, four luxury cars, two of them foreign, had been stolen from various homes in Montevista and Slope Ranch. One of them had been recovered. Two of the owners' homes had been burglarized. The recovered car had a set of duplicate keys in the starter-ignition switch and on the recovered car key ring there had also been a duplicate key to the house that had been burglarized.

"How does that read out to you?" he asked.

"Valet parking. The customer leaves his keys in the car and the house key is too often on the same ring."

"Right! And some sharpie down at the station came to the same conclusion. The four owners had only one thing in common—they were all regular customers of Le Bon Appetit. They never nailed Chico for it, but he was fired."

"And Pete Chavez replaced him. Didn't the boss at Le Bon Appetit know he was a friend of Chico's?"

"Apparently not."

"Juan told me this morning that Chico got Pete his job at the restaurant."

"In a way, he did. He probably told Pete there was a job open there."

That made sense. I asked, "Any new rumbles down here?"

He shook his head. "None I've heard of. I'm holding my thumbs."

"We'll need more than that," I said.

"We?" He shook his head. "Count me out. It's the Brotherhood's war, not mine."

"Orlando," I said, "when they involve the kids, either side, it's our war—against both sides."

"Speak for yourself," he told me. "I don't live in Montevista. I live here, right in the middle of the battle zone. And remember that I've got a police record."

I couldn't argue with that.

He smiled. "But I can be your stoolie."

"Fair enough. I think I'll go over and talk with Señor Ricardo Cortez."

He said, "You'd better leave that hot rod of yours parked here where I can keep an eye on it."

I walked the short block to the Brotherhood headquarters. The north side of the building was charred and blackened, but it didn't look like seven thousand dollar damage to me. The media thrives on hyperbole. There was a police car parked in front, a uniformed officer sitting in the passenger's seat.

His partner came out as I went in. Cortez was standing near the doorway, frowning.

"More trouble?" I asked.

"With the police? Always! What brings you down here, Mr. Callahan?"

"The same as last time—Peter Chavez. This Chico Ruiz the police are holding is a friend of his, isn't he?"

He shook his head. "Not any more. And the police are no longer holding Chico. He was at a picnic at Barnard Grove when the fire started. A dozen witnesses will testify to that."

I smiled.

He glared at me. "And none of them are liars."

"I'm sure they aren't. How about the other boy, the one they are holding for the fire here?"

"He has been released on bail. You might ask your friend, Sergeant Kranski, who it was that put up the bail money."

"Sergeant Kranski is not a friend of mine."

It was his turn to smile.

"I am not a liar, Mr. Cortez, any more than your friends are. What is Kranski's interest in Chico Ruiz?"

He shrugged. "I can only guess that he thought he could find Peter through him. Did you enjoy your dinner at the sergeant's home Saturday night?"

I stared at him. "Who told you that? Am I being followed?"

"Of course not! The niece of one of our members works for the Kranskis. Mrs. Kranski hired her before she was married."

"I see. Mr. Cortez, I am not the enemy. A man of your years should be able to distinguish between friends and enemies."

He smiled. "If I hadn't, I wouldn't be standing here. But as I told you before, amigo, the problem is ours and we will deal with it." He turned his back on me and went to his office.

I went to the station. Bernie wasn't in his office. Only Sergeant Ethel Wingram was in the office she shared with Kranski. He wouldn't be back until this afternoon, she told me.

"I came for information," I explained to her, "and possibly you can help me. I wondered who posted the bond for that boy who was being held, Fidel Carrero. Unless, of course, that's restricted information?"

"Not to a friend of Karl's," she said. "It was a man named Tony—" She frowned. "Tony something. I could look it up."

"Tony Toledo?"

"That's it."

"Do you have his address?"

She shook her head. "Only a post office box number. Would that do you any good?"

"I'm afraid not. Thank you for your help."

"I'll be sure to tell Karl you dropped in," she said. "He told me how famous you are. Weren't you with the Dodgers?"

"No, ma'am. The Rams."

"Oh," she said, her disappointment obvious.

I had met worse in my time. An incipient starlet in Glitter Gulch had once asked me if it was true that I had kicked the winning field goal against the Lakers in the World Series. How fleeting is fame. . . .

It was still early enough to get me home for lunch in time to avoid Mrs. Casey's disapproval. I took the left lane on the freeway.

Juan was out in front, knocking a tennis ball around the yard with one of Jan's discarded putters.

He was all smiles. "Pete phoned me!" he said.

"Good! From where?"

"I don't know. From out of town, he said. He's working in a garage. He's making sixteen dollars an hour! When he saves enough, we're going to get an apartment."

"Who told him you were here?"

"Father Murphy. Pete said he's glad I'm out of there."

"So am I. That's great news, Juan."

He nodded. "Maybe we can get an apartment with a pool. Sarah Felderstadt has one. I wonder if he phoned her, too?"

"You could call and ask her," I suggested.

He shook his head. "You do it."

I did it.

"Brock Callahan?" she said. "Of course I remember you. You're not easy to forget."

"You mean compared with the surfer?"

"He's long gone," she assured me. "What's on your mind? I hope it's carnal."

"Unfortunately, it isn't. Juan is staying with us now and his brother phoned him and told him he had landed a good job. Juan and I were wondering if he had phoned you."

"No. I doubt if he ever will. Is he working in town?"

"No. And he didn't tell Juan where he was calling from. That's kind of puzzling, don't you think?"

"Not for anybody who is a victim of a Kranski vendetta. Has that creep been over to talk with Juan?"

"Not yet. I warned him to stay away, but he's a stubborn man."

"And a horny one," she said. "The slob tried to come on with me. I told him if he showed up here one more time I'd phone his wife."

"That could put him on welfare. If Pete phones you, will you give me a call?"

"Of course. And then send up rockets."

Juan was looking at me hopefully.

"He hasn't phoned Sarah yet," I told him. "But he might."

"Maybe after he gets enough money, we can all be together?"

"Maybe," I said.

He went out to practice diving after lunch. Mrs. Casey went up to her boob tube daydreams. I put down in pen and ink all the people I had met and the things they had told me since my initial visit to the Tomorrow Club. I could remember them now; later, when it was more important, I might not. I had the gut feeling that there was going to be a lot of later in this war.

Juan was already up to half and full gainers and swan dives when I went out. Mrs. Casey had found him a book on diving. I joined him with my slightly-belly-flop straight dives.

We were reading again, poolside, when Jan came home. She studied us both, sighed, and went in to make our drinks.

When she brought them out, I asked, "Bad day?"

"Medium. Audrey is still harping about what she calls the Kranski account. She is beginning to sound like a damned banker. I suppose she means the *possible* Kranski account. I finally told her to shut up about it."

"I hope you didn't call her pushy."

"I came very close to it."

"You could open your own shop," I suggested.

"Don't be silly! Audrey is my very best friend!"

Juan gave me a puzzled look. I shrugged.

"Male chauvinists, both of you," Jan said. "And how was your day, boys?"

"Great," Juan said. "My brother phoned me. He has a good job, somewhere."

We gave her the details of that and then it was time for dinner.

The really bad news of the day came on the local tube after dinner. Chico Ruiz had been found dead in the dry gulch below the Andropolus house. He had been shot in the middle of the forehead, Mafia style. The spokesman for the sheriff's department held the opinion that Chico had not been shot there. He had been shot somewhere else—and dumped there.

Your move, Brotherhood.

8

PETER CHAVEZ WAS alive; that much Juan and I now knew. He was also working. There would be no reason for him to lie about that. But if he had, as he claimed, been working out of town, why hadn't he named the town? It would put him outside of Kranski's jurisdiction. It was possible that he had lied about that.

Orlando had decided to sit out this war. There was no sensible reason why I shouldn't follow his example. Neither side considered me an ally; I was the outsider, the intruder. And, as I stated earlier, some kids can't be saved.

I was still wavering in indecision next morning when Stan Nowicki phoned.

"Remember me?" he asked.

"I do. I suppose you're running out of money again."

"We're always running out of money," he said, "but that isn't why I called. It's not your money we're after this time. It's your investigative skills."

"Could you be more explicit?"

"Over lunch, I could. I'll buy."

"Save your money," I told him. "I can come down now."

"I knew you would," he said.

Stanley Paul Nowicki was one of the few lawyers I had known that I respected. It is a prejudiced view, of course, but bolstered by my move to San Valdesto.

Stan was an attorney for the ACLU, I had met him on my first case in this town.

He is a young and intense man with warm brown eyes, and an appearance that had given many prosecutors the mistaken impression that they were up against a patsy.

He was talking in Spanish to a heavy woman in his cubicle office in their converted storefront on lower Main Street when I entered.

She left a few minutes later and I went in.

"Our savior!" he said.

"Cut the con," I told him. "Why am I here?"

"In the interests of justice, of course. Sit down and smile."

I sat down.

"Did you hear about what happened to Chico Ruiz?" he asked.

I nodded.

"They're holding Fidel Carrero for that," he said. "The kid that was out on bail on the Brotherhood arson. And the DA thinks he has a case."

"But you don't?"

"I don't. Not with a gun. A knife—?" He shrugged. "Maybe. But not with a gun."

"Oh, boy! I hope you don't expect to feed that to a jury."

"I don't. I need more. They pulled in Chico, you might know, for that fire up in the hills."

"I know. And released him. He had all those witnesses who claimed he was at a picnic in Barnard Grove when the fire started. Kinsmen, no doubt?"

He shrugged. "Possibly."

"Then why was he killed?" I asked. "The way I read it, he was killed because somebody didn't believe he was innocent. Somebody who probably works for Chris

Andropolus. Do you know that one of Andropolus's boys put up the bail for the other arsonist charge?"

He nodded. "Tony Toledo. Where'd you learn that?"

"At the station. I've been looking for Peter Chavez for his brother Juan and I got involved in this civil war. I'm sure that Carrero isn't the only young Chicano who has signed up with Andropolus. And I am also sure that you should let him stay in jail for a while. You can call it protective custody. He's a hell of a lot safer there than out on the streets where the Brotherhood's long knives can get to him."

"That's the definitive word, 'knives,' Brock. Chico was *shot* and dumped in the same gulley where he was supposed to have started the fire. That's more Mafia than Chicano. How did that body get there? Fidel has no car."

"I'm sure he has friends with cars. A jury would know that."

"I suppose. For all I know, the DA has a weaker case than I have. But Chief Harris and his buddy Kranski are probably pressuring him. They're both supergringos. God damn that Kranski!"

"You're berating a kinsman," I reminded him.

"All Poles," he said stiffly, "are not red-neck bigots. We were victims of bigotry, ourselves, for decades."

"Toledo bailed Carrero out on the arson charge. Isn't Andropolus going to pay for his defense on this one?"

"Not to us. I have a hunch he's not going to pay for any attorney. They'll let the kid take the rap."

"Do you have Toledo's address?" I asked.

He nodded. "Why?"

"I thought I might run over there under an assumed name and tell him I am working for you and could use anything he might have to support Carrero's innocence."

"That's not honest, Brock."

"Neither is he. I can't use my real name. He knows it, but I doubt if he's ever seen me."

"And what if he checks with me? Am I supposed to lie?"

"You'll have to decide that."

"Okay," he agreed. "But don't play it heavy with him. You could get hurt."

"So could he," I pointed out.

The address was on Seaside Drive, a street that ran along the bluff above the beach. It was an upper middle-class area, close to the higher class area of Slope Ranch.

687 Seaside Drive was a green stucco house with yellow brick trim. It was on a corner lot, with a well-manicured dichondra lawn bordering on both streets.

A small, thin, black woman in a gray dress answered my ring. I told her I was Arthur Scott, an investigator for the American Civil Liberties Union and asked if I could speak with either Mr. or Mrs. Toledo.

"Wait here and I'll find out," she told me.

Several minutes later she came back to lead me down a long hallway to the rear of the house and through a door that led to the backyard.

There was a minuscule pool set in the big lawn and a sauna adjoining it. A well-tanned and long-limbed blonde in a sparse swim suit was sitting in a deck chair on the lawn reading a paperback romance novel. She lacked the mammaries to make a *Playboy* centerfold, but she would have commanded top dollar as a Vegas call girl. She looked up and smiled as I came closer.

I smiled back at her. "Is your husband home?"

She shook her head. "Does he have to be?"

My natural savoir faire deserted me. I answered with a schoolboy shrug.

"What did you want to talk to Tony about?" she asked.

"About a young man the police are holding on a murder charge. One of the attorneys in our office is defending him and he thought your husband might have some information that would strengthen our case."

"He should be home for lunch any minute now," she said. "Sit down, Mr. Scott."

I sat on a redwood bench nearby.

"Have you lived here long?" she asked.

"Three years. I came here from Los Angeles."

"So did we. This town is really dullsville, isn't it?"

"It's not Los Angeles," I agreed.

"Are you married?"

"Yes. My wife and I were married up here."

She looked past me then and said, "Here's Tony now, Mr. Scott."

I turned to see a fairly tall and very handsome, dark-complected man in yellow slacks and a green cashmere jacket coming from the house. I stood up.

His wife said, "This is Arthur Scott, Tony. He's an investigator for some lawyer in town."

"Like hell he is! He's Brock Callahan. Didn't you recognize his voice?"

She nodded and smiled. "But I didn't want to scare him away." She looked at me. "Tony was furious about that nasty thing you said about the stunt man."

"I apologize," I said. "It was cruel and thoughtless."

"What the hell do you want now?" Tony asked. "Are you still looking for that Chavez character?"

I shook my head. "I really am working for a lawyer, for Stan Nowicki of the ACLU. He's defending Fidel Carrero. He thought that you might have some information on Fidel that would help our case."

"Why would he think that?"

"You posted his bail," I said.

His wife said, "You never told *me* that, Tony."

"Mavis," he said firmly, "stay out of this!"

She stood up. "Yes, dear. Should I tell Delia that there will be three for lunch?"

He glared at her. She winked at me and went to the house.

Tony took a deep breath. "We've been checking you out, Callahan. You were a peeper down in L.A. after you left the Rams, weren't you?"

"Yes."

"And then you inherited a wad from some relative. But you still have to play cop. Why?"

"I got bored. Tony, I wasn't lying about Chavez. It's Sergeant Kranski I'm trying to protect him from. And I'm not lying about trying to get some helpful information for Nowicki. You can phone him if you want to. He'll confirm it."

He studied me for a few seconds. Then, "Okay, this much I'll tell you. I bailed out Fidel because he didn't set that fire. But on this murder rap I'm not so sure. You know what hotheads those Spiks can be."

"Chicanos," I corrected him.

"Whatever," he said.

"I'll accept hothead. And that should scare you, unless you're dumber than you look. Yours isn't the first Anglo gang to invade their turf. Some pretty rough characters have died trying to."

"I know. And now I'll say good-bye. I'm sorry you can't stay for lunch."

"So am I," I agreed. "That Mavis sure is a stunner."

"Go!" he said

"I'm going," I said, and went.

I had been denied lunch with Mavis and it was too late now to alert Mrs. Casey. I stopped in at Hannah's Hamburger Heaven for a cheeseburger and a pineapple milk shake.

"I know," Tony had said when I had told him the fate of the Andropolus predecessors. Crafty Chris had managed to circumvent that threat by signing up the malcontents among the underprivileged. And had, by that ploy, made both Kranski and Chief Harris his unwilling allies.

I went down to the station from Hannah's to shoot the breeze with Vogel. He was knee deep in paper work.

He looked up and asked, "Business or pleasure?"

"Business," I decided.

"I can give you five minutes." He pointed at the papers on his desk. "There's another four hours of work there."

I said, "I've been wondering how much of a case the DA has on Fidel Carrero."

He shrugged. "At a reasonable guess, less than he thinks he needs, but maybe as much as Kranski and Harris think he needs. I can't tell you any more than that."

"You're the homicide ace here. How come you're not involved?"

He frowned. "I'm not following you."

"If Carrero isn't guilty, somebody else is. Who's working on that?"

"Easy, Brock! Our immediate priority is trying to keep that lower Main Street pot from bubbling over. The area is crawling with officers." He pointed at the papers again. "Those are the reports I'm sifting through. And as of right now young Carrero is in the safest place in town. And *nobody* is going to railroad him."

"How young is he?" I asked.

"Fifteen. Ruiz was seventeen."

"Jesus!"

"Yes. Lock your doors tonight. This thing could spread."

I had planned to report back to Nowicki, but a phone call would serve as well. I went home.

A note on the kitchen counter informed me that Mrs. Casey and Juan were at a Little League ball game at Neville Park. Mrs. Casey's afternoon drama addiction must have been in remission if she could take her foster son to a ball game. It would be a sad day in this house when (and if) Peter Chavez came to reclaim his brother.

I phoned the ACLU office to report to Nowicki but was told he was in court and would be there the rest of the afternoon. I added the gist of the Toledo dialogue to my record and wondered how many others of Tony's kind had been brought up here by Andropolus. It didn't seem reasonable that Andropolus could hope to take over by working solely with juveniles.

It did seem reasonable that if one of the immigrants had killed Chico Ruiz, letting young Carrero take the rap would be a smart, if callous, move. Kranski couldn't have just picked that name out of a hat; he could have been furnished some fraudulent evidence by the newcomers. Apparently, it was not enough to please the DA.

And then another thought hit me. Pete had not told Juan the name of his new town, simply that he was out of town. So was I, at the moment. So were all those people who lived north of the San Valdesto city limits in an unincorporated area called Omega. It was more than a suburb; the population was only a few thousand less than that of the city.

9

FIDEL CARRERO WAS now a lad without allies, a traitor to his own people, deserted by the hoodlums he had joined. Only the ACLU was on his side now. I was inclined to Nowicki's view that the murder of Chico Ruiz had not been the work of a fifteen-year-old boy. It was logical to guess that some senior member of the Brotherhood would be a more likely choice.

In the current attorneys' world of the big buck the ACLU still held to the small buck view that *everybody* was entitled to justice under the law. That included Commies, Nazis, militants, arsonists—even kids.

A survey by a Los Angeles man-in-the-street interviewer had revealed that a large majority of our citizens, when read our Bill of Rights, had believed it to be a Communist treatise. The ACLU didn't. That stubborn belief made them highly unpopular among the vast uninformed. They had a hard row to hoe.

Fernando Schultz had heard that Peter Chavez was now working for Andropolus. Unless Andropolus had gone into the garage business, or Peter had lied to his brother, Fernando had been misinformed. But it might be worth looking into.

The Omega Pirates, Juan informed me when he came home, had defeated the San Valdesto Cardinals, 32 to 28, on the Cardinal home field. He had given it some thought and decided what the Cardinals needed was better pitching.

"Have you ever played baseball?" I asked him.

He shook his head. "But I could if I wanted to."

I didn't argue the point.

Mrs. Casey held to the view that the Cardinals needed stronger hitting. They had a chance to tie it up in the last inning, she explained. They had the bases loaded with nobody out and the heart of the lineup coming to bat. They had failed to score.

I agreed with her that scoring only twenty-eight runs in a Little League game indicated a serious lack of Cardinal power at the plate.

Jan came home to tell me that the name of Lois Woolrick Kranski had never once been mentioned in the elegant confines of Kay Decor.

That was the news of their day, brought home to me. Jan didn't ask for the news of my day, for which I was grateful. Down these mean streets . . .

The five o'clock local news on the tube featured an interview with Chief Chandler Harris. He explained in his pompous prose that the recent editorial in the local *Chronicle* about the inadequate police protection "in a certain section of our town" had been both vicious and inaccurate. He added that he was seriously considering a libel suit against the paper for its spurious claim that "our loyal citizens of Spanish extraction and other minorities in the area" had been too often victims of police indifference, harassment and occasional brutality.

He finished with his Santa Claus smile and assured us that all was now restored to order in peaceful San Valdesto; the situation was well in hand.

Five minutes later, on the same telecast, the national news was interrupted by a special bulletin. Ricardo

Cortez, head honcho of the Brotherhood, had been fired at by an assailant in a passing car as he left the group's headquarters. There had been three shots. Two had missed; one slug had grazed his right arm.

Two misses and a near miss; Chris Andropolus must still be relying on raw recruits for his army. He could learn to his sorrow that soldiers with knives rarely miss.

Jan shook her head. "I will never understand why you go down there."

"Urban relief," I explained.

"Relief from what?"

"From suburban ennui."

It was Humphrey Bogart week on Mrs. Casey's favorite Los Angeles television station. She and Juan went up to watch that after dinner; Jan went into the den to watch a PBS program on the history of the zither. I stayed with my notes in the living room, trying with my serviceable but not exceptional brain and my unerring instincts to find a course of action that might absolve Fidel Carrero from the charge of murder.

Nothing I had recorded offered any clue. My best present hope, I decided, was to talk with Fidel.

I phoned Vogel at home to ask if that could be arranged.

"Why?" he asked.

"Because I have been hired by the lawyer who is defending him to investigate."

"You're working for Nowicki?"

"Yes. I know you don't like him and I can guess why."

"You're right about the first part. Now tell me the why."

"Because he kept some innocent men out of jail that you tried to put there."

"Bullshit! He kept some *guilty* men out of jail."

"Bernie, you are neither a judge nor a jury. But if you

don't want to cooperate, I'll be forced to go to Chief Harris. I had dinner with him Saturday night. But you are my friend."

"And you're crowding it. All right! I won't be here after eleven o'clock."

"I'll be there bright and early," I promised him.

Vogel had been joking that afternoon when he suggested I lock our doors at night. But I made the rounds of the house before going to bed, locking every door, wedging the sliding glass doors. It was one of those misty nights they feature in British mystery novels and I left the lawn lights on.

"My macho man has paranoia," Jan observed. "And how about poor Juan up there all alone?"

"His door is locked," I said. "And so is the garage door."

She sighed. "You've always had a touch of nyctophobia, haven't you?"

"Yes, ma'am," I said.

I didn't remind her that my policeman father had been murdered at night, murdered by a hoodlum. It is not easy to explain about the real world to interior decorators.

Mist was still drifting in from the ocean when I went down to the station. There Bernie suggested that we could use his office to talk with Fidel if I so desired.

I shook my head.

"Why not?"

"You know why not. Confidentiality. I'm representing his attorney. You're representing the police. And you know what Chicanos think of the police in this town."

"You win," he said wearily. "I've alerted the desk sergeant. I'm sure you don't want to put a murderer back on the streets."

"What I hope to do," I explained patiently, "is get the

real murderer off the streets. We've done that before, you and I, haven't we?"

"Yes," he admitted. "Good luck. Drop back here after you're through."

"Of course."

Fidel was in a holding cell next to the drunk tank. He was short and thin. He was wearing faded jeans and a T-shirt with the word *Rialtos* emblazoned in red across the front.

"My name is Brock Callahan," I opened. "I'm working with your attorney."

"Yeh? How come he's not with you?"

"I can arrange to have you phone him," I said, "if you think I'm a liar."

He shook his head. "I know who you are. You're a friend of Orlando Davis, right?"

"Right. Tell me, why do the police think you killed Chico Ruiz?"

"Because he knocked up my sister. I didn't kill him, but I'm glad he's dead."

"Is that the only reason?"

"No. They still think I started that fire at the Brotherhood."

"Did you?"

"Why would I? If the cops think I did it, how come they let me go?"

"Because a man named Tony Toledo bailed you out. Were you working for him, Fidel?"

"Ask Nowicki."

"I will. Aren't you wondering why Toledo didn't bail you out on this murder charge?"

He didn't answer.

"Fidel," I said, "I'm on your side, but you're not making it easy for me."

He said nothing.

"Do you know Peter Chavez?" I asked him.

He nodded. "He used to be a Rialto."

"Do you know where he is now?"

He shook his head.

"Is he working for Toledo, too?"

"I don't know who he's working for and I don't know where he is. Okay?"

"If that's all you have to tell me, okay. But let me tell you, tough guy, you're a lot safer right where you are now than you will be if you get bailed out. There could be some sharp knives waiting for you out there."

"They don't scare me," he said. "Nobody scares me."

Another Juan—though several steps down the intellectual ladder. I went back to report to Bernie. "I don't think," I told him, "that Fidel should be permitted bail."

"He won't be. Harris and Judge Barker and I agree on that."

"Do you have an address for his sister? Fidel claims that Chico made her pregnant."

"I know. The last report we had on her, she is hustling down in Los Angeles."

"A pregnant hustler?"

"She had an abortion. Her father threw her out of the house."

"Because she was pregnant?"

"Nope. Because of the abortion. Figure that one out."

"I can't," I said. "Not since I left the church. Has ballistics come up with anything on the gun that killed Chico?"

He shook his head. "We never recovered the slug. They're working now on the ones that were fired at Cortez yesterday. I doubt if they'll come up with anything." He sighed. "We're not dealing with amateurs any more. We're turning into another L.A."

"No way, Bernie!" I said. "Andropolus is still a bush leaguer. We're going to get that bastard."

"You sound like Kranski," he said. "I hope for his sake we get to Andropolus before he does.

I left my car on the police parking lot and walked over to Rubio's Rendezvous. His cousin Manuel was behind the bar. Two tables in the place had been pushed together and seven of Rubio's kinsmen were sitting with him.

Ricardo Cortez sat at the far end. He said something I couldn't hear to the others and eight pairs of eyes swiveled my way. I felt like a visiting Martian.

"War council?" I asked Manuel.

He shrugged.

Rubio left his chair and came over to where I stood. He looked embarrassed. "Pancho," he said, "I—I mean it's—"

"A bad time to be here?" I asked.

He nodded. "Some other time?"

"Maybe," I said, "and maybe not."

I went out and down the block to see if Stan Nowicki was in his office. He was staring moodily out the big storefront window when I entered.

I told him about my dialogue with Toledo and Fidel's claim that Chico Ruiz was the father of his sister's aborted child.

"That's Fidel's story," he said, "and he's determined to stick with it. All he's doing is giving the prosecution ammunition. He is one stubborn boy."

"Isn't it true?"

"I don't know. I've got three people willing to testify they were intimate with the girl at the same time."

"Kids?" I asked.

"A boy of seventeen and two men in their late twenties. When I told Fidel that he went right through the roof."

"I am sure you also informed the prosecution."

"I did."

"And Fidel has no alibi?"

He shook his head. "The medical examiner couldn't pinpoint the exact time of death. And another thing the prosecution has going for them—Fidel *thought* Chico was the father. That's motive enough, no matter what the facts are."

"But no witnesses? That's not much of a case for the prosecution."

"With the mood of the town what it is right now? And if we get an all-Anglo jury?"

"Stan," I said, "we both know you would never agree to that."

"I won't. But how am I going to know which of Fidel's compadres are on his side and which aren't?"

"I'm sure you'll find a way," I said.

The phone rang then and he answered it. He said, "Yes, this is Stanley Nowicki." A pause. "I see." A pause. "Yes, I'll be here the rest of the morning."

He hung up and looked at me. "That was Ricardo Cortez. Do you know who he is?"

I nodded.

"He's coming here with Fidel's father. The father has agreed to confess to the murder of Chico Ruiz if I will defend him. It is comforting to know that the Brotherhood has finally decided to go the legal route, isn't it?"

I smiled. "And why? Fidel's papa had a choice, didn't he? He could take his chances with a jury or die in the street."

"That's cynical," he said.

"Is it? And was his motive wrath at what happened to the daughter he threw out of the house or was he working for Andropolus, as his son was?"

"I have no idea," he said.

"I do," I said. "And now I'll leave. Cortez has already glared at me today. Once is enough."

"Where was that?" he asked.

I told him.

"Well," he said, "your job is over here and now you can get back to golf."

"Not yet," I said. "I have another client, one who pays the same as you do—Orlando Davis."

"Thanks for your time, Brock. You are a citizen."

"And a sucker," I added.

10

I WAS WALKING back to my car on the police department lot when I saw Cortez and another man on the other side of the street. They were undoubtedly heading for the meeting with Nowicki. The man with Cortez was one of the men who had been sitting at the table.

It had not been, as I had thought, a council of war. It had been a seven man jury. Mr. Carrero had accepted the lesser sentence, and picked the best criminal defense lawyer in town.

Orlando was out in front of the club, talking with a youth of about eighteen. The youth shook hands with him and walked over to a beautifully restored 1931 Model A Ford De Luxe Phaeton as I came up the walk.

"Another mechanic has left us," Orlando greeted me. "He tried to tell me that he had an offer of sixteen dollars an hour."

"That's what Pete Chavez told Juan he was making," I said.

"Where?"

"He didn't say. Only that it was out of town."

"Something smells fishy, Brock. This kid said it was a garage connected with Corinthian Auto Supply. They don't have a garage out there. Just the parts store."

"Out where?"

"That new store in Omega. In the old Fedmart building. Corinthian, what does that mean?"

"Something Greek, I think. Isn't there a Greek city named Corinth?"

He shrugged. "How would I know? I majored in football at college." He frowned. "Hey, wait—Andropolus—"

"Is Greek," I agreed. "But so is Omega. It's a Greek letter."

"*That*," he said, "even I know. But do you know of any other stores out there with Greek names?"

"Orlando," I told him, "you're clutching at straws. Anything new to report?"

"Only what I just told you," he said coolly, "which you are too busy to look into."

"Don't sulk. I'll go out there right now and give it a look into."

He smiled. "I knew you would!"

Out of town didn't mean another town; the same thought had occurred to me. But stores don't pay their clerks sixteen dollars an hour. I took the freeway to the Northrup exit and Northrup Avenue to the former Fedmart building.

The entire front of the store had been re-faced in imitation lannon stone. The sign behind the glass of the front door assured the potential customers that all major credit cards were accepted.

Both new and used parts were available here. But, unlike most automobile supply stores, the used parts section was at least four times as large as the new.

Four barrel carburetors, blowers, twin tuned tailpipes, extra high voltage coils, magnetos, Pirelli racing tires; the used parts section was more speed shop than supply store.

A partially bald, thin and pallid man in a blue shop coat asked, "Can I be of service, sir?"

"I hope so," I told him. "A young mechanic who has

always worked on my car has left the shop. He told his boss he had a much better offer from you people. I was wondering where your garage is."

"We have no garage, only the store," he said. "Perhaps he is working here as a clerk?"

"Only if you have clerks who earn sixteen dollars an hour."

He smiled and shook his head. "I'm the assistant manager and I don't earn that much. I think your young friend lied to his boss."

"Probably," I said. "You must get a lot of hot rod trade here."

He nodded. "That and the sports car buffs. I worked at the Pep Boys store downtown for twelve years. They don't stock anything like this. There isn't an auto store in the county that does and none I've ever heard of in L.A."

"It should be a gold mine," I said.

He sighed. "I hope so. I'm not sure that Manny, Moe, and Jack would welcome me back."

Sixteen dollars an hour at forty hours a week multiplied by fifty-two weeks totaled thirty-three thousand, two hundred and eighty dollars a year. I had worked that out on my calculator last night. That should take a youth out of the low rent district. It could also put him into the no rent district, behind bars.

When I had grown up in Long Beach after my father died, the Long Beach Hot Rod Association had taken me and my roughneck friends off the streets and onto the drag strips. If, as Orlando thought, Andropolus was running this store, he could reverse that trend.

Street kids must know there had to be a reason somebody was paying them that kind of money. And a man who had spent twelve years with the Pep Boys would have to wonder where Corinthian was getting used parts as glistening as these. There weren't that many recent model cars junked each year. He also had to know that the components needed to build a complete car would cost at least twenty times as much, if bought separately, as the completed car.

Some mechanics repair and some dismantle. Some kids work on cars and some steal them. Drugs and gambling and prostitution were apparently not enough for Andropolus. He had added a youth movement.

Would the dismantling shop, I wondered, be in Santa Maria, where Chavez had last been seen? That was an improbable choice. The expensive cars were here in San Valdesto, both foreign and domestic. A friend of mine who drove a Rolls Royce had recently paid two hundred dollars for a wheel cover. Four of those could be stolen in a few minutes by any twelve-year-old with a screwdriver.

I phoned Orlando from the fast food joint across the street from the store after I had eaten. I told him what I had learned and what I suspected.

"But how do we find the garage?" I asked.

"There's a way," he said, "but I'm afraid to suggest it."

"A stakeout of the loading platform?" I guessed.

"Right! Somebody has to deliver the stuff to the store. And then you could tail the truck back to the garage."

"What if the truck makes only one delivery a week?"

"It could happen," he admitted. "That's why I was afraid to suggest it."

"Maybe we could hire some low-cost help."

"Not my boys, if that's what you're thinking. Two of them have probably joined the enemy. I don't want the others to get hurt."

"We'll talk about it later, Orlando. I'll run over and get a look at the layout."

My car was still on the lot adjoining the store, at the street end of it. There was a narrow strip of the lot that was not open to parking. It extended to the back of the store. There was no platform; the receiving area was at ground level.

Surveillance of the area would be easy from the parking lot at this end. Anyone sitting in a car on the lot would not be likely to arouse suspicion in the receiving area.

I moved my car to the rear of the lot and kept my eagle eye on a blue panel truck. It stayed where it was. About forty-five minutes later a green panel truck drove in and the driver began to unload.

There was no reason to follow it when it left. The lettering on the side identified it as a local wholesaler of auto parts, a firm that had been in business here for decades. The driver was obviously delivering to the new parts section of the store; everything he carried in was boxed and labeled.

The blue truck was still parked when I drove home an hour later.

The afternoon paper was on the front lawn. I took it out to the back, where Juan was sitting and reading.

"Aren't there any kids around here?" he asked me.

"Not many. Are you getting bored?"

"All these books are the same," he said. "The good guys always win."

"What's wrong with that? Would you rather see the bad guys win?"

"At the Shelter, they did."

"Would you like to go back there?"

He shook his head.

"Juan," I explained, "in books for young people, the good guys always win. When you get older you can read some books where the bad guys win. Would you like to learn to play baseball?"

"Maybe," he said. "Yes."

"I'll take you out to the Omega Boys' Club tomorrow. They're starting an instructional league."

He went back to his book. I read the paper. Fidel had been released; his father had confessed. In his statement to the press, Chief Chandler Harris explained that the recent addition of more police officers to the area had been responsible for the speedy apprehension of the killer.

The Brotherhood would be amused to hear that.

Juan was in the pool and I was dozing when Jan came home. She asked me, "Do you know a woman named Shirley Andropolus?"

"I met her once. She's Sergeant Kranski's niece. And her husband is our local vice king."

"Oh, God! She told me Lois Kranski had recommended us. I'd better phone Audrey."

"Why?"

"Don't be silly! What if word gets around that Kay Decor—" She didn't finish. She went back into the house to phone Audrey.

She looked even more unhappy when she came back. "Do you know what that dopey Audrey said?"

"Not yet. But I'm sure you're going to tell me."

"She said that I shouldn't get hysterical. She said that I shouldn't jump to conclusions. She said we weren't in this business for our health. She said we would talk it over sensibly tomorrow after I had cooled down."

"That's old dopey Audrey for you. But her advice is sound. Cool it, kid. Let me make you a drink."

"A triple bourbon over ice," she ordered. "No water!"

"Jan—!"

"Get it," she said.

I didn't make her a triple. I made her a double in a big glass and put a lot of ice into it. That made it look like a triple. I made mine slightly weaker.

We sat in silence for a few minutes, watching Juan swim, before I suggested, "One thing you could do is explain to your other clients that you accepted the Andropolus account as a favor to the former Lois Woolrick."

"It wouldn't work," she said.

Juan swam another length of the pool.

"Well," she admitted, "maybe it would."

All was again peaceful in the Casey-Callahan-Chavez household. The sun went down, the moon came up. Mrs. Casey and Juan went to her room after dinner for another Bogart classic, Jan into the den for a PBS program on ancient Mayan architecture. I phoned Nowicki at home and asked him if he could find out for me who owned Corinthian Auto Supply.

"I could," he said. "So could you. All you would have to do is phone the store and ask them."

"It might alert them," I explained. "I have a gut feeling that they're crooked."

He promised he would check into it.

The moon went down, the sun came up. I took Juan out to the Boys' Club in Omega after breakfast. The baseball coach lived in Montevista, and he told me he would bring Juan home.

An hour after that, Nowicki phoned. Corinthian Auto Supply, he informed me, was a subsidiary of Corinth Enterprises. The president of the firm was Christopher Andropolus.

11

CORINTH ENTERPRISES, that was an innocuous name for a bush league hoodlum front. The major league Mafia must have dozens of them. Our local and famous medical clinic was a mecca for the ailing from Las Vegas, but they didn't stay over.

So far as I knew. . . .

Juan's parents had deserted him. Peter was his last best hope. Peter was already in violation of probation and seemed to be heading for even more trouble with the law. If he was working at a legitimate garage, he would have told Juan that. If the garage was out of town, he would have named the town.

The rich get richer; the poor have to hustle. There was no doubt left in my mind; Peter must know he was dismantling stolen cars. An expensive attorney might convince a sympathetic jury that he didn't know. But poor people can't afford expensive attorneys. Andropolus had failed to provide one for Fidel.

These were the thoughts I carried down to Stan Nowicki.

He smiled. "Maybe Ricardo Cortez would be a quicker solution."

"No!"

"A little joke and a bad one," he admitted. "But if we found Pete and got him out before the police closed in on him—?"

"And then he would fink on the boss? No way!"

"That wasn't my thought. My thought was we might build a strong case on the claim that as soon as Pete suspected the cars were stolen he quit."

"That would be a lie, Stan."

His smile was cynical this time. "I didn't mean to shock you, a former Los Angeles private eye. I'm sure *you* have never lied."

I said coolly, "There were times in my trade when I found it necessary to lie."

"I rest my case," he said.

I drove to the Tomorrow Club. Orlando was in his office, doing some paper work—for a change.

"Spying again?" he asked.

"You have a long and vindictive memory," I told him.

He nodded. "So do you. What's on your mind?"

I gave him the information I had picked up at Corinthian Auto Supply and what Stan had learned about the parent company and its president. I added what Stan had suggested as a course of action.

"To point out the obvious," he said, "we can't find Pete until we learn where he is."

"True. I was thinking, on the way here, that maybe Pete and the young man who deserted you yesterday might not be the only ones who were offered jobs."

"There's one more," he said. "But he turned it down. I'm sure he doesn't know where the place is. And I'm even surer he wouldn't want to get involved in this war. Not after what happened to his father. He's Ricardo Cortez's oldest son."

I put my disappointed look on my face.

He sighed. "Don't pout. He's in the shop now. I'll ask him."

Five minutes later he came back with a bulky young man who was almost a prototype of his father, lacking only the gray-streaked beard and the white eyebrows. Ricardo Cortez, Junior.

Orlando must have briefed him in the shop. He said, "I don't know where that garage is."

"Couldn't you call the man who approached you and tell him you've changed your mind?"

He shook his head. "I don't know his name. Pete Chavez recommended me." He paused. "Mr. Callahan, Pete and Fidel and Chico and I were all Rialtos at one time and friends. Now Chico is dead, Fidel's father is in jail, and Pete is being hunted by the police. I don't want to get mixed up in all that. I'm married and I have a two-year-old son."

"It might help to put away the man or men who tried to kill your father," I pointed out.

He was silent for seconds. Then, "I'm sorry. The police will have to take care of that."

I couldn't resent his rejection; he was being a citizen. "I understand," I told him.

When he left, I told Orlando, "You trained him well."

"Too well," he said. "Another dead end. I wish these kids were more like you and me."

"What do you mean?"

"Vindictive," he said, "and tricky."

"Speak for yourself, con man. I'm going home."

The dead end opened when I got home. Mrs. Casey informed me that a Sarah Felderstadt had phoned and asked that I call her back.

"I'm playing the fink," Sarah told me, "and it might cost me my lover. Pete phoned me. He wanted to know if there was any way he could see Juan without your finding out about it. He's coming here this afternoon."

"Did he tell you he's working for Chris Andropolus and that he's involved in a stolen car operation?"

"Dear God, no! What should I do?"

"Tell him he can see Juan. He'll be home at two o'clock and I'll bring him over to your place."

"And then you'll leave?"

"No."

"Callahan, be reasonable! Do you want me to wind up with another surfer?"

"No. And I don't want Pete to wind up in the can. Trust me, Sarah."

"I do. It's that pukey Kranski I'm worried about."

"Don't be. You can always phone his wife and tell her the move he tried to make on you. If that doesn't work, I guarantee you I can handle him."

A silence on the line and then, "Okay."

When I hung up, Mrs. Casey asked, "Has something happened to Juan?"

"Not that I know of. Why?"

"You mentioned his name."

"Pour yourself a glass of Irish," I said, "and I'll have a touch of American corn and we can discuss it over lunch. Peter Chavez wants to see his brother."

"Does that mean Juan will be leaving us?"

"We'll discuss it over lunch," I repeated.

I gave her a sanitized version of the situation over our Irish stew. Her frown deepened as my story continued.

When I had finished, she asked, "Is this brother of Juan's still in the church?"

"I don't know. Juan is. Maybe, like me, Peter still follows the teaching of the church without attending Mass."

She shook her head. "It's not the same."

I didn't argue with her. The look on her face convinced me that it would be best to drop the subject.

Baseball, Juan told me when he came home, was not as easy to learn as swimming.

"I know. If you didn't enjoy it, you don't have to stay with it. It's a team sport, Juan. And that is a very important thing to learn."

"I guess," he agreed. "I'll stay with it."

I gave him the good news and his face lit up. "Are they going to get married? Am I going to live with them?"

"Let's go over and find out," I said.

When I rang the S. Felderstadt bell at apartment 5, 747 Alvaro street, the two middle-aged women in terry cloth robes were still playing gin rummy at the far end of the archway that led to the pool.

Sarah was wearing slacks as glistening black as her hair and a white silk blouse.

"Juan!" she said.

"Hi," he said. "Is Pete here?"

"Not yet. Don't I get a kiss?"

"I'm not a baby," he said.

She kissed the top of his head. "Come in. Pete should be here soon."

It had to be a furnished apartment; I was sure Sarah's taste was not this gauche, bleached, discount house moderne. I sat on a studio couch, Juan in a chair where he could watch the door.

I looked at Sarah and she at me and Juan looked at the door. After a minute or so, Sarah said, "There could be fireworks."

"Hothead?" I asked.

"At times. This might be one of them."

She opened the door to him a few minutes later, a stocky young man in jeans and a T-shirt. He smiled at Juan and then looked at me.

"Don't blame Sarah," I told him. "It was my idea."

"It's okay," he said. "I checked you out with Orlando

before I came here. Are you still running that Spelke Mustang?"

I nodded.

He went over to ruffle Juan's hair.

Sarah said, "Juan, Mr. Callahan and Pete have some things they want to talk about that might be boring to us. Would you like to go out to the pool? Can you swim?"

"Of course!" he said.

A swim suit for him was easily arranged; he wore the bottom of one of Sarah's bikinis.

Pete sat in the chair Juan had vacated. "A lecture?" he asked.

I shook my head. "I'm not qualified. I suppose you know what's been happening in town?"

That, he told me, was why he had quit the garage this morning. "I'm not Mr. Clean. I've always hustled. And I could con myself into believing that working on cars was my trade. Where they came from was none of my business. Then there were those fires and Chico got killed and Mr. Cortez got shot at. I couldn't con myself after that."

"And you couldn't desert your own people," I added.

"Maybe," he admitted, "down there in me somewhere. What I plan to do now is go back to work with Orlando. Sarah is going to get a part-time afternoon job and still work the dinner trade at the restaurant." He paused. "That means there will be nobody home for Juan. I wondered, if we paid you board, could you keep him with you until Sarah can quit the afternoon job?"

"Of course. No need for pay. I'd pay you to have him around for a while. Let him stay here today and bring him over to the house tonight."

"Thanks. Thanks a lot."

"I suppose," I said, "you're still not ready to play the fink?"

"What do you mean?"

"To tell me where that garage is located."

"Not yet," he said. "As soon as this buddy of mine gets out of there, I will. The rest of those so-called mechanics that work there were brought up from Los Angeles. They ran the same kind of chop shop down there, but they didn't have a store. I'd turn them in right now. But not my friend."

"Does your friend drive a 1931 Model A Ford DeLuxe Phaeton?"

He nodded. "Do you know him?"

I shook my head. "Only his car. I don't want to know his name. Did Tony Toledo hire you?"

"No. A guy named George Culver. He's from L.A., too. He could be the Greek's muscle man."

They would bring Juan back after they had dinner—around seven o'clock. I relayed the information to Juan and Sarah and stopped in to see Bernie on the way back to the house. He was in court again, the sergeant told me, and would go right home from there.

Mrs. Casey was waiting for me at the open front door when I came home. "Where is Juan?" she asked.

"He'll be here after dinner," I assured her.

"For how long?"

"Until his brother and his girl friend can save enough for one of them to be home during the day."

"Girl friend—? You mean they're not married?"

"Not yet."

"I won't have it!" she said.

"You won't have what?"

"Juan living with a pair of adulterers."

I wanted to tell her it was none of her business and

there wasn't a damned thing she could do about it. But where could I find another like her?

I added the day's revelations to the record and got myself a bottle of Einlicher, a soothing potion for a busy day. I was dozing when Jan came home.

She looked at the empty beer bottle and said, "I see you've already had your drink. I'll make my own."

I withheld my comment, as I had with Mrs. Casey.

When she came back to the den I told her where Juan was and why.

"No wonder Mrs. Casey looks so gloomy," she said. "What kind of person is this Peter Chavez?"

"Sounder and smarter than I anticipated. The people I had talked with gave me some mixed reviews on him."

"You're going to miss Juan when he leaves, aren't you?"

"Yes."

"So am I," she admitted. "Maybe we should consider—"

"No," I interrupted.

We sat in silence, except for the sound of Mrs. Casey grumbling to herself in the kitchen.

There was very little dialogue at dinner. Sarah and Pete brought Juan home as we were having our coffee. He didn't look happy.

"It's only for a little while, Juan," I told him.

He nodded.

They left and he went to Mrs. Casey's room to share another Bogart adventure.

Jan said, "Sarah is more than pretty. She's beautiful!"

"Inside and outside," I agreed. "Is there anything worth watching on the tube?"

She shook her head. "Let's play some gin rummy."

I forget who won; our thoughts were elsewhere. Juan went to bed. We watched the ten o'clock local news on the tube and went to bed. It was a while before we fell asleep.

It was the news report on the radio we listened to at breakfast that brought the grim news of the day. Christopher Andropolus had been found dead in the study of his Montevista home.

The preliminary investigation by the Sheriff's department indicated that he had scuffled with somebody, fallen, and crushed his temple on the corner of the desk in the room.

His wife had been visiting a friend in Lompoc. There were several suspects in the case; their names were being withheld by the department, pending further investigation.

12

"I SUPPOSE THAT's not bad news to you," Jan said.

"It could be. The war could get hotter. I'm sure neither side is going to surrender."

The phone rang. It was Pete Chavez. His buddy was now back at the club, working for Orlando. The chop shop, he told me, was off Lorimar Road but it couldn't be seen from the road. It was a cement block building with no address. It was called Crazy Jerry's, though he didn't know why. "That," he said, "should take some of the wind out of Andropolus."

"He doesn't have any left," I told him. "Haven't you heard? He was murdered last night."

"Jesus!" he said. "Now it starts."

"My thought exactly. Thanks, Pete."

I phoned the sheriff's department and asked for Sheriff McClune.

When I identified myself, he said, "I suppose you're going to tell me there's another poker game at Vogel's house tomorrow night."

"No." I relayed the information Pete had given me.

"Are you sure of this?"

"Yes."

"Who's your source?"

"A former worker there I will not name. He was working for me on an investigation I'm on. But I'm not going to put his neck on the line for the Andropolus gang."

"Okay, you bullheaded bastard. But this had better be solid."

"If it isn't, you can sue me," I told him. "I'll keep you in court for the rest of your life."

"I'm sure you would," he admitted. "Thanks, Brock."

When I came back to the table I asked Jan, "Have you ever heard of a place called Crazy Jerry's?"

She had, through her local historian, Audrey Kay. Some kook named Jerry something had built it when the Second World War started, a solid place of concrete and steel. He had stocked it with enough dried food to last him for years. He was certain that the Germans were going to win the war; this would be his hideaway.

Jan shook her head. "People!"

"People," I agreed.

It would be comforting to believe that the death of Chris Andropolus and the imminent raid on Crazy Jerry's would convince the intruders that they had come to the wrong town. But I tended to agree with Pete Chavez; the worst was yet to come. Chris Andropolus wouldn't have moved up here simply to start an auto parts store. Toledo's visit to Rubio's Rendezvous was proof enough of that.

The coach of the instructional league team at the Boys' Club had told Juan he would pick him up from now on and bring him home. I drove down to the station.

I went in to see Kranski first. I told him, "Pete Chavez is back in town. He gave me some information that should shut down that dismantling shop Andropolus was running. Did you know about the place?"

"Only rumors," he said. "Where's Pete? I want to talk with him."

"No, you don't. He was working for me. I've already given Sheriff McClune the information. Pete did both you and him a favor."

"To hell with that! And if you withheld information about his whereabouts, you could be in trouble, too."

"Not as much trouble as you'll be in if I tell Lois you tried to make time with Sarah Felderstadt."

He glared at me. "If she told you that, she's a damned liar!"

I smiled at him. "Kraz, don't play the village virgin with me. Some of your old teammates have told me what a cock hound you are. I'll bet Chief Harris would be surprised to hear that. He's a moral majority man."

"You bastard!" he said.

"You haven't even skimmed the depth of my bastardry," I assured him. "Have a good day."

From there I went to Vogel's office. He was in, for a change. I related the events of the morning and my dialogue with Kranski.

"Brock, remember he is one vindictive son-of-a-bitch."

"I know."

"Of course," he said, "compared with you—"

"He's Peter Pan. Do you know a man named George Culver?"

"I sure do.Where did you run into him?"

"I haven't yet. He's the man who hired Chavez."

"He's really heavy," Bernie said. "We got his record from L.A. Assault, conspiracy to commit murder, drugs, pandering. And all they ever nailed him for was pandering, when he was a lot younger. He walked on the others. He'll probably take over, now that Andropolus is dead."

"Who were those unnamed suspects I heard about on the radio this morning?"

"There's only one left," he told me. "Ricardo Cortez.

The DA assured me that homicide's work will be light on this one. He said they caught him red-handed."

"Which means—?"

"He was at the house when it happened. The DA didn't tell me much more. I haven't heard Cortez's side of the story yet, but I will." He sighed and shook his head. "I thought a couple days ago that things were starting to quiet down. But with this Culver here—"

"One game at a time, Bernie. Culver's next."

"Oy!" he said. "Jocks!"

"Would it be possible," I asked, "for me to talk with Cortez?"

"Not this morning. But your good friend Stanley Nowicki is his attorney. He should have the story by now."

A uniformed man came in then to tell Vogel that the chief wanted to see him in his office. I drove over to the ACLU.

Only the volunteer secretary was in the office. Mr. Nowicki, she told me, would not be in until late this afternoon.

I had one possible source of information left. I drove over to the Tomorrow Club. Orlando told me young Cortez, Ricardo, Jr., had left for home half an hour ago, but he had talked for quite a while with Pete Chavez and Pete was still in the shop.

Pete had the story. Andropolus had phoned the senior Cortez and told him he was not responsible for the man who had shot at him. He knew who the men were but it was not information he intended to give the police. Cortez should know by now, he had pointed out, that the law was not friendly to either side in this war. And then he had suggested a truce, and asked Cortez to his house to discuss it.

The door was partly open when Cortez got there, but

he rang the bell—just as the sheriff's black-and-white came up the driveway. McClune's office had been alerted by an anonymous phone call.

"He was jobbed," Pete said.

"Maybe. Unless some neighbor heard the commotion?"

He shook his head. "I doubt it. And how much investigation do you think Sheriff McClune and Chief Harris are going to put into this?"

"Don't compare those two, Pete. Sheriff McClune is a first class police officer."

"For gringos, maybe." He grinned. "Nothing personal."

"Well, I'll go and have a talk with McClune. He owes me for the information of yours I fed him. And, incidentally, I told Sergeant Kranski this morning that he had better not heckle you. I used some leverage I had on him. And I also told him that you were working for me as an undercover investigator at the chop shop."

"Thanks, Mr. Callahan."

"You can call me Pancho," I said.

The sheriff's station was on the far side of town from where I was, out in Omega. I took the freeway.

McClune was being interviewed by some local and big city string reporters when I got there. According to his secretary, the raid on Crazy Jerry's roost had been successful.

"But I know he'll be glad to see you," she said. "He should be available in a few minutes."

He was available half an hour later. He had a big smile for me. "Did you come for your good citizen award?" he asked.

I shook my head. "I came here in the interests of Ricardo Cortez. I wondered if you agree with me that he might have been framed?"

"It's possible," he admitted. "But I'm not sure Chief Harris would agree. We're working with the city on this. The DA seems to think he has a cinch case."

"He would," I said. "He and Harris are spiritual twins."

He smiled again. "You sound like Stan Nowicki. Are you working for him?"

"Partly. But mostly for myself and Ricardo."

"Well, Vogel will be working at the city end. That's where Ricardo lived. I'm putting our best man on our end. I'm sure you'll agree that Vogel is the best man they have in town."

"And consequently overworked," I pointed out. "I was thinking that maybe you could give me some official status."

"You figure I owe you?"

I nodded.

He sighed. "So do I. Brock, don't play it heavy now. I'll back you, if you need it, but not on anything heavy."

"I will be all finesse and discretion," I assured him.

"Get out of here," he said. "*But keep us informed*!"

"Of course," I said.

It was only a few minutes short of noon, too late for me to alert Mrs. Casey that I would be home for lunch. I drove over to the Boys' Club, less than a mile away, and took Juan to lunch at a nearby Denny's.

He was pretty good on batting he told me, but not too hot on catching.

"It takes time, Juan. I wasn't very good on catching, either. That's why I turned to football when I was young. At least you now have some kids to play with."

He nodded. "How come there aren't any in your neighborhood?"

"Most of them are out of town, at summer camp. The

rest of the year many of them go to private schools out of town."

"It's different in my neighborhood," he said. "It's the parents who leave town. Why do they have us if they don't want us?"

I shrugged.

"How come you don't have any kids?" he asked.

"Because I couldn't afford them until it was too late. You're going to visit us once in a while after you move, aren't you?"

He nodded again. "You can be my make-believe uncle."

If it hadn't been for my macho, chauvinistic false pride, Jan had told me, we could have a couple of kids by now. . . .

I took Juan back to the Boys Club and drove down to Rubio's Rendezvous. There were only two patrons in the place, drinking red wine and arguing in Spanish.

"No lectures," Rubio said. "Not today."

"That's not why I'm here. I've just come from a talk with Sheriff McClune. I suggested to him that Ricardo could have been framed."

"Any damned fool knows that," he said. "Even Sheriff McClune."

"What we know and what we can prove are not the same, Rubio. I hope to prove it."

"You're going to work on this?"

I nodded.

"I apologize for my rudeness," he said. "Beer?"

"Coffee. Do you know a man named George Culver?"

"I have heard of him. I have never met him." He poured my coffee. "Is he the new Andropolus?"

"I don't know. What did you hear about him?"

"That he's tougher than Andropolus and smarter than Toledo. Nowicki told me that."

"The police have his record from L.A.," I said. "Nowicki could be right."

"The police!" he said. "What do they know? What do they care?"

I didn't rise to the bait. I sipped my coffee.

He asked, "Did you hear about that raid at Crazy Jerry's?"

"Yes. I'm the one who alerted McClune about the place. That's the main reason he's letting me work with him."

"Well," Rubio said, "I admit he's fairer than Chief Harris. But who isn't?"

"Vogel will be working the town end," I said. "He's smarter than both of them—and fair."

"Yes," he admitted. "He's a good friend of yours, isn't he?"

"Quite often. Do you have an address for this Culver?"

He shook his head. "But I can get it. Pancho, be careful!"

"I will if you will."

"It's not your war," he said.

"Yes, it is. As I told your friend Ricardo Cortez, this is not his town or my town. It's *our* town."

He smiled. "Let's not argue. The coffee is on the house."

Nowicki, I had been informed this morning, would not be in his office until late in the afternoon. I went home and filled in my record for the day.

The hunt for Peter Chavez was over. So was Kranski's vendetta against Chris Andropolus. But the war went on.

Juan should be home soon. I put on my trunks and waited for him. Maybe he could teach me how to execute a swan dive.

13

SARAH PHONED AROUND four o'clock and asked if she and Pete could come and get Juan and keep him over the weekend. I told her that was a good idea and then went to the kitchen to inform Mrs. Casey. I didn't want their visit to be a surprise to her.

"I have no comment," she said coolly.

"They're real nice people," I told her. "I'm sure you'll like them when you meet them."

"I don't intend to meet them," she said.

I considered explaining that her stubborn attitude might offend Juan, but decided I was already on thin ice. Losing Juan was bad enough; losing Mrs. Casey would be a disaster.

Jan came home before they arrived and I explained the situation to her.

"I'll get his clothes ready," she said. "You fix me a drink."

Which we both did.

Over our drinks, she suggested, "Maybe we could meet them out on the front lawn—if you can think of a reason for being out there."

I told her what Juan had told me; he wasn't too good on catching. "I could be out there throwing a baseball to him," I said, "and you could be watching us. But we don't have a baseball."

"We have some old tennis balls," she said. "I'll get one."

And that was the way we staged it, in deference to Mrs. Casey.

As we walked back to the house, Jan said, "You and Juan were right. She is a classic beauty!"

"She's young," I pointed out. "I'll bet when you were—"

"Not on my best day," she said.

It was a quiet dinner. Mrs. Casey had no words, Jan and I very few.

Mrs. Casey went up to her room after dinner, I to a new Elmore Leonard novel, and Jan to matching more drapery, upholstery, and carpeting samples on the dining room table.

At ten o'clock Jan and I watched the local news on the tube. The important news of the day we already knew; Ricardo Cortez was in custody for the murder of Christopher Andropolus. The other suspects had been released.

We went to bed before the program was over.

Neither Orlando nor Nowicki nor Vogel worked on Saturdays; I had no place to go. Jan went to work. I had another cup of coffee and read more of the morning paper than I wanted to know. I was still there when Mrs. Casey came down to make her breakfast.

I folded the papers on the breakfast nook table for her, preparing to leave her domain.

"I apologize, Mr. Callahan," she said.

"For what?"

"For the way I've been acting. After what you did for my niece and all—My late husband used to tell me I was more Catholic than the Pope. But the church has been my solace through some very difficult times."

"Mrs. Casey," I assured her, "I admire and envy your

faith. It carried my mother through some difficult times, too. There are many ways you remind me of her. That's one of the reasons I love you."

"Aagh, you!" she said. Her eyes were wet and she sniffled. "Thank God you're still Irish."

I had been granted partial absolution. I blew her a kiss and went back to my notes.

There was no pattern showing there. And then I remembered that I had told Peter it was possible some neighbor had overheard the fracas in the Andropolus house and phoned the sheriff.

But, if my memory was sound, there had been no houses close to his on my trip up there.

I got in the car and made my second trip to the Andropolus hilltop home. My memory had been sound; there was no house within hearable range. I went past to the nearest driveway on the opposite slope and turned back.

There had been two cars on the Andropolus driveway when I went by on the way up, a Camaro and a Mercedes. On the return trip three women were standing and conversing next to the Mercedes.

I recognized two of them immediately—Lois Kranski and Shirley Andropolus. The third took a few seconds of memory search before I recognized her—the tanned, long-legged, platinum blonde, Mavis Toledo.

They couldn't be planning the funeral service for Chris; last night's obituary page in the paper had stated that there would be neither a funeral nor a memorial service for him. He had been cremated and his ashes would be shipped back to his native Greece.

Was Lois Woolrick Kranski finally being introduced to the real world?

I had my answer about five minutes after I got back home. A Mercedes pulled into our driveway and she got out. She stood next to the car in apparent indecision. She was still standing there when I went out to greet her.

"Am I intruding?" she asked. "Are you busy?"

"Not at all. Come in."

"I've just had a disturbing talk with some friends," she explained as we walked toward the house.

"Mavis Toledo and Shirley Andropolus?" I asked.

She stopped walking and stared at me. "How do you know that?"

I told her how I knew and why I had driven past.

"I see," she said. "And then I remembered the argument you and I had at our house. You must think I'm a real nitwit."

"Nope. Only badly misinformed. Let's go in and talk."

We went into the living room. She sat on the couch, I on a chair across from her. The reason Shirley had gone to Lompoc to stay with friends, she told me, was that she had suspected Chris had been involved with another woman and confronted him with it. He had become abusive and she had left.

Mavis had told her about a man named George Culver. "Do you know anything about him?" she asked.

"Only his Los Angeles police record."

"Mavis told me he and Chris were partners in Los Angeles. And that Culver had never approved of that car stealing ring. Did you read about that, that place off Lorimar road that was raided?"

"Yes."

"Mavis thinks Chris and this Culver may have argued about that. And now it looks as if perhaps Culver was the one who told the sheriff about the place."

"It wasn't," I said.

"How do you know?"

"I'd rather not say."

She was silent. I had the feeling there was more she

wanted to tell me. I asked, "Would you tell the police what you've just told me?"

She shook her head. "It's all supposition. But you could tell them, couldn't you?"

"I could. Is that all you want to tell me?"

"No. But the rest is not something I want you to tell the police."

"I'm not the police, Lois. And I don't tell them everything I learn. It will be our secret."

On the night Chris had been killed, she told me, Kranski had gone to his weekly poker game at a friend's house. About an hour after he had left, their water heater had started to leak. She had phoned the friend's house to ask Karl how to turn off the main water supply. Karl was not at the game.

"And you know Karl's temper," she said, "and how much he hated Chris."

I nodded. "Did you ask his friend about any previous poker games?"

She frowned. "Why would I?"

"Can't you guess? I would have asked."

She stared at me. "You're not suggesting a—another woman?"

"I will only say I would have asked. And if you give me the friend's name, I will."

"Are you implying that Karl is an adulterer?"

"Lois," I said gently, "you implied he was a murderer."

"Yes," she admitted. "Dear God, yes!" She paused for a moment in indecision. Then, "His name is Einar Darbo. Do you know him?"

I knew him, a Kranski prototype, a sergeant who worked vice, another street cowboy. I nodded.

"If Karl should find out I've been checking on him—" she said.

"He must know you have. Didn't you ask him where he had been when he came home?"

"Yes. And he told me he had gone down to the station to pick up some paperwork he had forgotten to bring home. Captain Walsh had explained to him there that they were shorthanded that night and he had commandeered Karl to go along on some narcotic raid."

"And you didn't phone Captain Walsh to confirm the story?"

She shook her head. "Why would I?"

I didn't answer.

"I know what you're thinking," she said. "I'm naïve."

I smiled at her. "We're back where we started. I think of you as trusting."

Mrs. Casey came in then to ask if my visitor would like to stay for lunch. It was her Irish way of telling me that lunch was ready, whether I was or not. We were back to normal.

Lois shook her head and thanked her for the offer. I walked to the door with her. There she told me, "You do what you think best about this, Brock. Karl told me that your teammates used to call you The Rock. I can understand why."

I didn't explain to her that it was a nickname converted from what they had called me my rookie year—Rockhead.

Over our pre-lunch libations, Mrs. Casey asked, "Is Mrs. Kranski one of the Woolricks from Boston?"

"Yes."

"She seems nice."

"She is."

"She comes from a bad tribe," Mrs. Casey said. "They were snooty, crooked Protestants."

"The worst kind," I agreed. "Almost as bad as fallen Catholics."

She didn't dispute that. She changed the subject. "Don't you miss Juan?"

"I do."

"I was wondering," she said, "if maybe you could phone his brother and suggest that they take Juan to Mass tomorrow?"

"Right after lunch," I promised.

Which I did. Sarah answered and told me that Juan and Pete were out at the pool. She gave me the further information that Juan had convinced them that all three of them should attend Mass tomorrow.

When I relayed the good news to Mrs. Casey she asked, "Felderstadt isn't an Irish name, is it?"

"I doubt it."

"Well," she admitted, "she's almost pretty enough to be Irish."

"Maybe she's Polish, like the Pope. When did you see her?"

"When I happened to glance out the living room window."

"Tomorrow, when they bring Juan back, I'll introduce you."

"I look forward to it," she said.

She had said the same about the visit from Father Murphy. I hoped it wasn't for the same reason.

I looked up the phone number of Sergeant Einar Darbo and called him. The woman who answered the phone told me he was working; he would be home around two-thirty. I gave her my name and phone number and asked that he call me back.

A few minutes after two o'clock I got that nervous, housebound feeling and drove out to Omega, to the home of Sergeant Darbo. It was a standard California one-story, stucco tract house in a neighborhood of look-alikes. I parked across the street from it.

About fifteen minutes later a high-wheeled, four wheel drive pickup truck came rolling down the street and turned into the Darbo driveway. I got out when he did and met him on his gray front lawn.

He was a big man, a Scandinavian from Minnesota, with ice blue eyes and close-cropped blond hair. "Callahan" he said. "What's with you, peeper?"

"Just a few questions."

"About what?"

"Karl Kranski."

"I can see where you're heading," he said. "No comment." He brushed past me and took several steps toward the house.

"All right," I said. "I'll talk with Captain Walsh."

He turned. "What the hell does that mean?"

"Kranski claims Walsh commandeered him for a narcotics bust the night of the poker game—the same night Andropolus was killed."

Darbo shook his head. "That dumb Polack!"

"The way I see it, Einar, better he should be guilty of adultery than of murder. I wondered if he had missed some Thursday nights before that."

"Why don't you ask him?"

"Because he's not only dumb, he's bullheaded."

"That's for sure." He looked down at the lawn and back at me. "Kranski has *never* been to one of our poker games. But if you tell anybody I told you that I'll call you a liar."

"Do you know the name of the woman?"

"No. I swear to you I don't. And that's God's honest truth."

I thanked him and left.

There wouldn't be any point in asking Captain Walsh

if Kranski's story was true. His veracity was already discredited. But I didn't intend to tell Lois what Darbo had told me and what we both suspected. Not yet. I had stopped taking adultery cases when I left Los Angeles. Murder was my present concern.

14

THE FACT THAT Karl had never attended the poker sessions at Darbo's house didn't automatically prove that his alibi this time was for the same adulterous reason. Nor was it a certainty that any of his Thursday night excursions were adulterous. But, considering his record, it seemed to be a logical guess and Darbo had as much as confirmed it.

One thing the good ol' boys loved to brag (and lie) about were their carnal conquests. Darbo had sworn he didn't know the name of the woman. I was not on familiar terms with any of Kranski's other buddies. Maybe Vogel was. Vogel suffered fools gladly—if they played poker.

The evening paper had an item in the financial section that stated Anthony Toledo, a former resident of Los Angeles, had recently joined the local stock brokerage office of Abbot and Clarke. It didn't seem possible that it could be the same Toledo. That was the firm where I dealt. I phoned Dick Abbot at home and asked him if this was the Toledo who lived at 687 Seaside Drive.

"Yes," he said. "Why?"

"I just wondered. I met him at a party a couple nights ago."

"It's the same man," Dick said. "He worked for us in Los Angeles when I was down there. And while I have you on the line, Brock, I firmly believe you should think seriously of increasing your holdings in Amicor International. They've just—"

"I have guests, Dick," I interrupted him. "I'll probably be downtown Monday and maybe we can talk about it then."

Dick Abbot was the son of the man who had founded the firm in Los Angeles, the dullard son of an intelligent father. Obviously, he had neglected to do further research on the employment record of Anthony Toledo. I could help him with that on Monday.

A Juan-less Saturday passed without further incident. Sunday morning dawned chilly and windy.

"No golf today," Jan decided for us at breakfast. "It will be even windier out on the course."

She stayed with the paper after breakfast. I went out for a run, all the way to the Andropolus house. There were no cars on the Andropolus driveway, only two morning papers and a throwaway advertising sheet. The house had a deserted look.

It was still far short of lunchtime when I finished showering. I drove down to the station and asked my friend, the desk sergeant, if I could talk with Ricardo Cortez.

Ricardo was sitting on his bunk, staring at the floor, when the turnkey let me in. He looked up and tried to smile. "My son told me of your interest," he said.

"It's our town," I reminded him. "Do you agree now?"

He sighed and nodded.

"Tell me how it was," I said. "I heard it secondhand."

Here is the way it was: Andropolus had explained to him on the phone that he was no longer interested in the penny ante loot they were getting out of his neighborhood, not with the trouble it had caused him. They were moving into the richer sections of town. It had not been his men who had shot at Ricardo; he was sure he could find out who they were. He had suggested a truce and explained that he was subject to night blindness and his wife was not at home to drive him to Ricardo's house. But he would come tomorrow, if Ricardo agreed. Or Ricardo could come to his house tonight.

"And you went."

"I am a damned fool!" he admitted.

"Do you think he was telling the truth about those men who shot at you?"

He shrugged.

"It's possible," I suggested. "The kids are fighting each other. But so are some of the adults in the Brotherhood. Mr. Carrero admitted he shot Chico."

"Mr. Carrero," he said stiffly, "was *never* in the Brotherhood. And he is a sick man. I am sure he lied to keep his son out of the gas chamber. Fidel has many more years left than his father has."

"I'll probably be working with Lieutenant Vogel on this," I told him. "He's the best man the department has."

He nodded in agreement. He took a deep breath. "This is the first Sunday in fourteen years that I have missed Mass."

It had been longer than that for me. Maybe too long.

When Jan is home, Mrs. Casey and I never have a drink before lunch. It was Jan who suggested it today. We didn't have Juan to brighten the meal.

Sarah and Pete brought him home before dinner. Pete was working nights again on the Le Bon Appetit parking lot to pad out his Tomorrow Club wages. He and Sarah both worked the dinner trade on Sunday.

Mrs. Casey was still wearing her churchgoing best when they arrived and her demeanor matched her attire. Sarah promised her that Juan would attend Mass every

Sunday he spent at their place. She didn't promise that she and Pete would and Mrs. Casey didn't suggest it.

I had the feeling that she didn't give a damn what they did, but that could be a product of my agnostic cynicism.

I walked to their car with them when they left. There Peter told me, "Rick and I and a couple of other former Rialtos want to help you clear his father. They don't trust the police, so I'll be their funnel to you."

"They can trust Lieutenant Vogel," I said.

He shook his head. "Only you."

"Okay," I agreed. "But what if Rick's father is guilty?"

"He isn't," he said. "And we both know it."

"That's true," I lied.

I asked Juan at dinner if he'd had a good time.

It had been great, he told me, even if their pool was too small. He had advanced from "I could if I wanted to" to "their pool is too small." He had joined the upwardly mobile set.

He and Mrs. Casey went to her room after dinner to watch a Spencer Tracy memorial special, Jan to her beloved PBS. I tried to frame in my mind the words I would use to convince Dick Abbot that he should not employ Tony Toledo. Trying to explain chicanery to a stockbroker could be as difficult as trying to explain anti-Semitism to Adolf Hitler.

I didn't get a chance to use the words I had framed. The receptionist at Abbot and Clarke informed me next morning that Dick Abbot was home with the twenty-four-hour flu.

I walked along the row of cubicle offices to the last one, the one that housed Anthony Toledo. He was alone at his desk and his door was ajar. I went in.

He looked up and smiled. "I can guess why you're here. When Dick phoned me last night he mentioned that you had asked about me." He paused. "Could I state my case?"

"It should be interesting," I said, and sat in his customer's chair.

He had worked for three and a half years in Abbot and Clarke's Beverly Hills office, he told me, servicing the carriage trade. He had taken over the Chris Andropolus account when one of the other brokers had retired. In the months that followed he had invested Chris's money wisely in a rising market. They had become friends. One night, at a party in the Andropolus house, Chris had pointed out that many of his guests were sniffing cocaine; it was the "in" thing. And he had pointed out further that there was a lot more money in supplying that trade than the commissions Toledo was earning (and sharing) with Abbot and Clarke.

That was how it had started and Chris hadn't lied; they did very well. Until Chris had brought Culver, an old friend, into the action.

"Chris didn't have a record and neither did I," he said. "But Culver did, and the Beverly Hills Police Department knew it."

The heat was on. It was Culver who suggested they move into another high rent district. Scottsdale, Arizona had panned out as an inhospitable area; they had decided on San Valdesto.

"I don't suppose," I said, "you would tell the local law what you just told me."

He shook his head. "I'm solvent. I don't need this job. But I don't plan to get on Culver's hit list. And I like this town."

"What made you think Rubio's Rendezvous was in the high rent district?"

"I didn't. And neither did Chris. He and Culver argued about that."

"And the chop shop?"

He shrugged. "That could have been Chris's idea. He was a car freak. He drove a Clinet."

"Maybe they argued about that. Maybe they even fought."

He shook his head again. "If you're suggesting George killed Chris—no way! They were like brothers. Culver's mother was Greek."

"Can you think of a likelier suspect?"

"Two," he said. "Ricardo Cortez and Sergeant Kranski." He smiled. "So that is my sordid story, which I will deny I ever told you. I plan to stay in town, whether I work here or not. I'm sure I can find other employment here. As for Dick Abbot, he was getting a reputation as a churner in Beverly Hills. That could be why his papa sent him up here. Any more questions?"

"Just one. What do you know about Amicor International?"

"Very little," he said, "but I could look it up. One thing I can tell you now is that Abbot and Clarke underwrote more than we've been able to sell so far. Some of the boys are pushing it, but Dick hasn't told me to—not yet."

"And cocaine?" I asked. "Are you still pushing that?"

"No. As I explained, I am a solvent citizen now, the same as you. Have a good day, Mr. Callahan."

I went out almost admiring the bastard. He knew when to lie and when not to lie. It had taken me years to learn that in Los Angeles.

I drove to the station from there and Bernie was in. I told him most of what I had learned since we had last talked.

He said, "I find it hard to think of Kranski as a Lothario."

"That was his reputation in Dallas. Was there a narcotic raid the night Andropolus was killed?"

He shook his head. "We haven't had one for a month. Did you get anything worth repeating from Toledo?"

"Only the sad story of his lost innocence. And his choices for the murder—Cortez and Kranski."

"We've been concentrating on Culver," he said, "and came up with nothing. The DA thinks he's got enough to nail Cortez."

"We know why, don't we? Oh, one more thing, Shirley Andropolus suspects her late husband was traveling the same wife-cheating road her uncle is. They had a fuss about it and that's why she went to visit her friends in Lompoc."

"Which gives us another suspect," Bernie said. "But I doubt if Mrs. Andropolus could have knocked her husband down. What I can't figure—who phoned the sheriff's department? Culver would seem to be the logical suspect for that. It got Cortez out of his hair."

"According to Toledo, Culver and Andropolus were very close friends. Culver's address isn't in the phone book. Do you have it?"

He nodded. "Why?"

"I thought I could play the welcome wagon game again, the way I did with Andropolus."

"Not yet," he said. "We've got Culver under surveillance."

"Well, maybe you could tell me the names of some of Kranski's friends. I'm sure you don't want your fellow officers to know *you're* investigating him for murder."

"Outside of Darbo and Harris," he said, "the only one I can think of is Gus Jankowski, and he's on vacation."

I shook my head. "I bring you meat. You give me crumbs. Thanks for nothing, Loot."

"Don't sulk," he consoled me. "You can always play golf."

"Sure! And let Cortez get jobbed."

"Easy, buddy!" he said. "The officers in this department are not all Kranskis."

There are enough of them, I wanted to say, but didn't.

I went from there to Nowicki's office. He wasn't in. At the Tomorrow Club I was told that Orlando was out on a field trip with some of the younger members.

I went home and added the day's discoveries to my record and had lunch with Mrs. Casey. I was sitting and sulking after lunch when Bernie phoned.

He told me the surveillance on Culver had ended. "Don't tell him you're working for us," he warned. "I haven't cleared it with Harris." He gave me the address.

"I'm not working for you at that address," I said coolly. "It's in the county and I've already been cleared there by Sheriff McClune."

"Ain't you somethin'?" he said. "Good luck, Lochinvar."

I had seen the Culver driveway before, but not the house. The driveway was the one on the opposite slope where I had turned around after driving past the Andropolus place.

The house wasn't visible until I had made the second of three turns on the long driveway. The view of it from the road was screened by a row of tall eucalyptus trees. It was a redwood house with a graveled roof set into the side of the slope. The view of the Santa Ynez Valley from his parking area was impressive.

The man who opened the door to my ring was on the impressive side, too, tall and wide and bulky. His face was pugnacious, except for his warm brown eyes. He was wearing cords and a T-shirt and sheepskin lined slippers.

"Mr. Culver?" I asked.

He nodded.

"My name is Brock Callahan," I said, "and—"

"I've heard of you," he said. "Come in."

The room he took me to was a small room about halfway down the long hall which led from the foyer. There was a desk in the room, a file cabinet, a computer on a low stand, and two chairs. I took one of the chairs, he the other.

"Chris and Shirley have told me about you," he said. "And I know you're a good friend of Sergeant Kranski's."

"First of all, I'm not a friend of Karl Kranski's. He and Harris and the DA seemed determined to nail Ricardo Cortez for the murder of your friend. Cortez is more my friend than any of those three."

"That's not the word I got," he said. "Go on."

"I've learned that Chris planned to divert your common interests from the low rent district to our area. At least, that's what Chris told Ricardo."

"According to Ricardo. Did it occur to you he might be lying?"

"About Chris phoning him or your switch to richer pastures?"

"Both."

"We've already confirmed that last part," I told him, "including your move to Scottsdale that didn't pan out. The Phoenix police told us that."

"Who is 'us' and who is 'we'?" he asked. "You're not a cop, are you, Callahan?"

"I'm working with them, county and city. You can phone McClune and Harris if you want to confirm that. Would you like me to recite your Los Angeles rap sheet?"

He shook his head. "I think it is time for you to leave. And you can tell your friend Kranski we know who his girl friend is and we might leak it to his friend Harris."

"Who is 'we'?" I asked. "You and who else?"

"Good-bye," he said. "Close the door on your way out."

There was a time in my spotted career when I would have floored him. But I was a solvent resident of suburbia now. I only slammed the door.

15

LOIS HAD SUSPECTED and Darbo had almost admitted that Kranski was involved with another woman. It would have been a violation of confidence if I had faced him with these accusations. But telling him what Culver had told me could be considered a warning. I drove down to the station.

He was in his office. But so was Sergeant Ethel Wingram.

"What's on your mind?" he asked me.

"It's—kind of private," I said.

Sergeant Wingram smiled and said, "If it's man talk I'll go out and have a cup of coffee. You'll answer my phone, won't you, Karl?"

He nodded.

She left and I told him about my visit to Culver's house and what he had told me.

It didn't seem to bother him. "So?" he said. "Did he tell you her name?"

I shook my head.

"And you believed that crap?"

"Shouldn't I have? I came to warn you, not to accuse you."

"You didn't answer my question," he said. "Did you believe it?"

"Don't get cute with me, Karl. I know your record. And you must know how stuffy Chief Harris would get about extramarital relations. I'm not here to heckle you."

"What were you doing at Culver's house?"

"I was warning him, just as I did you. It might be wise for you to realize that Ricardo isn't the only suspect in this killing. You probably hated Andropolus as much as he did."

"More," he admitted. "Maybe you and Vogel can make a case out of that. But you'll never sell it to the DA."

What a hardhead; it was like talking to a wall. I went out without saying good-bye.

Bernie wasn't in his office. I went home.

Juan was out in front, bouncing a tennis ball against the garage door and catching it on the return bounce.

"Move back a little," I told him. "That's too easy."

He moved back. He said, "I started a double play today."

"Coach has got you playing in the infield?"

He nodded. "But I'm not sure I'll stay there. The guy running to second stumbled and fell down."

"You've still got your hot bat," I consoled him. "If you wind up in the American League you could be a designated hitter."

He shook his head. "I don't like to sit on the bench. I want to *play*!"

I could have explained to him that designated hitters earn a lot of money. But it's not something you can explain to a true jock. They want to *play*.

Jan came home with the news that another friend of Lois Kranski's had dropped in at the shop, a woman named Mavis Toledo.

"She is also a friend of Shirley Andropolus," I told her. "And her husband used to work for Chris."

"Dear God!" she said. "Here we go again! Audrey told me her husband works for Abbot and Clarke."

"He does. I guess he decided he can afford to turn honest."

"Well, I'm not going to get into another fuss with Audrey. It's her shop and Mrs. Toledo can be her client. I already have more work than I can handle."

Dick Abbot phoned after dinner, the twenty-four-hour flu behind him. He said he was sorry to have missed me; Toledo had told him I had come to the office. Had I decided about Amicor International?

"Not yet," I told him firmly.

I didn't tell him that he should have investigated further on Toledo's employment record. Two pieces of bad news in one phone call might send him back to his sick bed. Nor did I mention his reputation as a churner in Beverly Hills; that had come from an unreliable source.

I had been planning for some time to switch to a discount broker. Not for the commission fee it would save, but for the nuisance I could avoid. Discount brokers don't make phone calls.

The ten o'clock news on the local TV station informed us that Ricardo Cortez had been indicted for the murder of Christopher Andropolus. The trial date was set for next Monday. Somebody was in a hurry.

I phoned Nowicki in the morning and he told me he would be in his office until noon. "Anything new to tell me?" he asked.

"Not enough to take into court next Monday. I'll be down there before you leave."

I stopped in at the station on the way down and recounted to Bernie my conversations with Culver and Kranski the day before.

"The man has paranoia," he said. "Why would we want to railroad him?"

I shrugged.

"Maybe we can get Culver to name the woman," he said. "Hell, it could be in his own interest."

"Not really," I pointed out. "It would serve as an alibi for Kranski. He probably used me as a messenger, figuring I'd tell Kranski. Threatening to tell could make Kranski nervous, but if Culver followed through to Harris, the threat is gone."

"Right." He sighed. "We're nowhere, aren't we?"

"So far. I'm going over to see Nowicki now. Maybe he's learned something we can use."

"I doubt it," he said.

Bernie was not in Nowicki's fan club. Stan had successfully defended too many criminals that Bernie had tried to put where he knew they belonged—in jail. Though he was a scholarly man, Bernie's regard for our constitutional rights had dimmed through his years on the mean streets.

He was right this time. Nowicki had learned less than I had. Nothing. I told him all that I had learned and what I suspected. We agreed it was not enough to take into court.

"And deep in my heart," Stan said, "I *know* Ricardo is not guilty."

"In your head, too?"

He smiled. "Let's stay with what we have, Brock. We've got more heart than sense. You work for nothing and I for a pittance."

To an attorney a pittance meant about twice as much as I had earned through my working years in Los Angeles. It's hard to feel sorry for lawyers.

Culver seemed to be Bernie's choice for number one.

I went to the Rendezvous to get Rubio's appraisal of that opinion.

"Maybe," he said. "I found out his address at the meeting last night. I phoned you an hour ago, but you weren't home."

"What meeting?" I asked.

"The Brotherhood," he explained. "His house is close to the Greek's."

"I know. I went there yesterday. He told me to get lost."

Rubio smiled. "He must be a very big man. Most of the Brothers still feel that Sergeant Kranski is the man we want. You know he hated Andropolus, don't you?"

I nodded. "And I know why."

"He is the man we have been watching. There is a woman he was involved with. One of our members tried to question her. She told him if he ever came back again she would tell the police that we were threatening her. She is a gringo. Who do you think the police would believe?"

"Another gringo," I suggested. "Do you have her address?"

"I can get it."

He went to the wall phone at the end of the bar. Two minutes later he came back with the address and her name. The address was in Omega.

It was in the general neighborhood of Einar Darbo's house, in an older section of the area. The houses were small and mostly stucco, but they were not look-alikes. Her house was white frame with a screened front porch.

The woman who answered the door had the same overall contours as Lois Kranski. But her hair was a badly bleached blonde and her eyes a vivid blue. She was wearing a red corduroy robe and matching corduroy slippers.

"Miss Benedict?" I asked.

She nodded.

"My name is Brock Callahan," I told her, "and—"

"Karl has mentioned you," she interrupted. "You're a friend of his, aren't you?"

"I try to be. It's not always easy. Could we talk?"

"Maybe. Did he send you?"

"No. But I'm here in his interest. It's not something I can explain to him."

"I can believe that. What do you mean—'his interest'?"

"He is a suspect in the murder of a local hoodlum," I explained. "A man named Chris Andropolus. Perhaps you read about it?"

She nodded. "Karl hated him. I thought some Mexican did that."

"That's the man who's been accused of it. It happened last Thursday night."

She stared at me. "And Karl claims he was here?"

I lied with a nod.

"That lying bastard!" she said. "He hasn't been here for three weeks. Are you a cop?"

"No. But some of my cop friends are concerned about Karl. They don't want him to be railroaded."

"Who'd do that? Some Mexican?"

"Possibly."

"One of them came here," she said, "and I told him off good. But I'm not going to lie for Karl Kranski. He wasn't here Thursday night or the two Thursdays before that. And you can tell him that I never want to see his ugly face again."

"I will," I promised. "Thank you for your cooperation."

"You're welcome. You married?"

I sighed. "Unfortunately, I am."

"Then stay away from my door," she said. "I got this thing for big men. But from now on they'd better be single."

"A very wise decision," I agreed. "Thank you again."

I had promised the lady I would be her messenger to Karl. Sergeant Wingram didn't have to take herself out for coffee today; she was not in the office.

"Jesus!" Karl said when I came in. "You again?"

I smiled at him. "Only for a few seconds. Flora Benedict asked me to tell you that she never wants to see your ugly face again. She's miffed because you missed the last three Thursday nights."

"God damn you! Whose side are you on?"

"The law's side, Karl. Aren't you?"

"You sanctimonious bastard! Get out of here!"

"Calm down, Kranski. I'm not going to tell Lois."

"I don't give a damn who you tell," he said. "Get out of here!"

I went to Bernie's office from there to tell him what I had learned. He wasn't in. It was time for lunch; I went to Rubio's for a big bowl of chili with corn chips and a beaker of Mexican beer.

I told him about my talk with Flora.

"*Three* Thursdays?" he said. "If it had been only last Thursday it would be more—you know—"

"Incriminating?"

"I guess that's the word."

"She could have been lying."

He shook his head. "If he only missed one night she would not have been that angry."

That made sense.

He asked, "Why is it that the police don't know about this Flora?"

I shrugged.

He answered for me. "Because they have Ricardo, that's why."

I said nothing.

"Pancho," he said, "we need you."

"Sad but true," I agreed.

I went to my other source from there. Orlando was in his office, eating a hero sandwich and washing it down with a can of beer.

"What's new, whitey?" he asked.

"That's what I came to ask you."

"I got nothing," he said. "I make a lousy stoolie, don't I?"

I told him most of what I had learned.

He made a face. "Lover boy Kranski? There must be a lot of desperate women in this town."

"In all towns," I said, "including Dallas. Is Pete Chavez in the shop?"

"He should be. Unless he went out for lunch."

He hadn't. He was bending over a Camaro engine with a stroboscope, checking the ignition timing.

He looked up and smiled. "How's Juan doing with the baseball?"

"Better. He was switched to the infield yesterday."

"He'll get the hang of it. That kid can be any damned thing he wants to be." He switched off the stroboscope and turned off the engine. "I guess it's time for lunch. I've got an extra sandwich, if you're hungry."

"No, thanks. I've got a bellyful of Rubio's chili. Have you or Rick learned anything?"

"Nothing solid. It's been quiet around here lately. I heard that Culver has decided to switch his action to your neighborhood."

"I heard the same. And another thing I heard was that Andropolus was the man who wanted the chop shop, but Culver didn't. But it was Culver who approached you."

He nodded. "Probably on orders from Andropolus. Chris didn't have Culver's muscle but he was the brains. He was the boss."

"Until now."

"Right."

"And Culver was his closest neighbor."

He stared at me. "I didn't know that. Are you thinking what I'm thinking?"

"Partly. Kranski seems to be the Brotherhood's choice."

He nodded. "Natch! They have reason to hate both of them. But Kranski never paid any Chicano sixteen dollars an hour."

16

JUAN CAME HOME with the news that he had been tried out at pitching today.

"How did you do?" I asked.

"I could have done better," he said, "but I didn't want to. Pitchers only play every fourth or fifth game."

"Relief pitchers play more often than that."

"They sit around a lot, too. Coach lent me a ball and glove to practice with. Would you throw me some bouncers?"

Right and left, low and high, I threw him grounders, some with rotation on them and some without. He missed very few.

"You look like an infielder to me," I told him.

"You should see those black guys," he said. "They're better athletes, aren't they?"

"Some are and some just try harder, just like the rest of us. The way it is, Juan, the best players get the best jobs in sports. That's not always true in other trades. In sports, it's not the people you know or the color of your skin. You get paid for what you deliver."

"I know *that*!" he said.

I should have known he knew that. It wasn't compassion that had finally brought the blacks into major league baseball; it was money. Winning teams are what keep their wealthy owners wealthy.

I threw him ten straight grounders, which he fielded

without error, and called off the practice session. My arm was getting tired. He stayed out there, bouncing a tennis ball against the garage door. I went in the house to add the day's discoveries to the record.

The way it was shaping up there were now four suspects for the death of Chris Andropolus. They were George Culver (proximity), Karl Kranski (family), Tony Toledo (history; the stunt man incident), and the police choice, Ricardo Cortez.

But why had Chris died? All four had the muscle; who had the motive? Motive, means, and opportunity; that's what a prosecutor needs to take into court. The DA must have felt certain that that deadly triplicate was tailored to fit only Cortez.

The possibility of Andropolus's having been killed by an intruder, a burglar, had never been considered. Nothing had been stolen.

Nowicki would undoubtedly try to get some Chicanos on the jury. The DA would undoubtedly protest if any of them were members of the Brotherhood. A jury of one's peers is honored more in theory than in practice.

The local afternoon paper reported that the Pep Boys had taken over the Corinthian Auto Supply building. It would be their Omega outlet. The former Pep Boy's assistant manager I had talked with would be the new manager for them. Manny, Moe, and Jack had not deserted their former employee. It would be unkind to assume that the previous manager had been in on the take but that is what I assumed.

Sherrif McClune phoned after dinner. "I'm glad you answered," he said sourly. "It means you're still living in the county. That is where Andropolus was killed, if you remember. And I hope you also remember the conversation we had in my office."

"I do. I've been giving Bernie Vogel what little I've

learned. I assumed he passed it on to your department. You told me that one of your deputies would be working with him."

"He was. But now Chief Harris seems to think the DA has the right man in Cortez. How about you?"

"I have a gut feeling that Ricardo was framed."

"So does one of my deputies. His name is Fran Sanchez. He told me he had worked with you before I came here. Do you remember him?"

"I sure do."

"Could he drop in and talk with you tonight?"

"I'll be home."

I had worked with Sergeant Francesco Sanchez on another case involving juveniles when I first moved to San Valdesto, the summer I coached a Little League team in Omega.

He was at our door half an hour later, a tall, slim, and bronzed man who could have played the town marshall in a western picture, a Chicano Gary Cooper.

"You've put on a little weight," he said.

"*Very* little. Come in."

Jan was again sorting samples in the dining room. We went into the den. He sat in my favorite chair in there and stretched out his long legs. He said, "I heard that Bernie's been given the word by lard-ass Harris. And I can guess why."

I shrugged.

"To think I almost went to work for the bastard when I got out of school!"

I said, "Let's get off the Harris kick, Fran."

"Yeh." He took a deep breath. "Bernie's been very cooperative up to now. He's the best man they have down there."

I nodded.

He smiled. "But, knowing how you operate, I figured there might have been some things you didn't pass on to him."

I stared at him.

"A little joke," he explained. "I apologize."

"Okay."

I got my notes from the desk and leafed through them. I related all that I had learned from the characters involved since I had played handball with Orlando. It took quite a while.

When I had finished, he said, "Bernie never told me about Kranski and this Flora Benedict. Maybe I ought to have a talk with her. Omega isn't in the city."

"You'd be wasting your time. What we want to know is where Kranski was the night Andropolus was killed."

His smile was cynical. "You're thinking like I am, aren't you? Kranski hated Andropolus."

"He did. But I'm not thinking like you are, not yet. At the risk of demeaning your kinsman, I don't feel that Ricardo is completely in the clear, not yet."

It was his turn to stare at me.

"You're a cop first, Fran," I reminded him. "Everything else is second. I'll grant you that Ricardo is my least likely suspect at the moment. But both of us could be wrong. Now, what do you have for me that I don't know?"

He reached into his jacket pocket and took out a small grayish silver metal button. He handed it to me. It was embossed with a five-pointed crown and the word Rex in barely readable type below the crown. There was a short length of black thread attached to it and a shred of gray cloth.

"Only McClune and I know about that," he told me. "We didn't give it to the city boys because we know what a big mouth media hound Harris is. It was in Andropolus's clenched hand. It's from a blazer made by a firm named Royal Valance, a British firm. Those jackets aren't available in town here. The closest source was two stores in Los Angeles."

"And why wouldn't you tell Vogel about this? I can't believe Ricardo Cortez would go to Los Angeles to buy a British blazer."

"Neither can I. But he used to visit his sister down in Westwood quite often and there was a store there that handled that line."

"Did you check with the store?"

He shook his head. "They went out of business four years ago and there were no customer records. Cortez's sister died two years ago. There was no customer record on Ricardo at the other two stores."

"Did anyone in Ricardo's family know about the blazer?"

"We didn't ask. He wasn't wearing one when we picked him up. There was no need to ask."

"I would guess that blazer is ashes by now."

"It could be. But it was only one of two buttons on each sleeve. Maybe it wasn't missed."

"Why didn't you tell the DA about this?"

"Because he's got as big a mouth as Harris. And if we gave it to Nowicki, he'd be obligated to tell the DA."

"You and McClune could be in big trouble, Fran. Police officers withholding evidence—?"

"Trouble is our business. We're not in business to give any murderer fair warning. I have to believe you agree with that."

"Guilty," I agreed.

"I'm sure you have more friends in the department

than you have downtown," he said, and stood up. "Keep in touch, huh?"

I nodded. I walked to the door with him. The mist was drifting in from the ocean, shrouding the lights in the house across the street.

"Nice night for a murder," he said. "Keep the faith, Irish."

"I'll try to. Drive carefully, amigo."

Jan was still in the dining room, going through some furniture catalogues. Juan was reading in the living room.

"Time for bed," I told him.

"One more chapter?" he asked.

"One more. Holler when you're ready. I'll walk to the garage with you."

"Why?"

"I need the air," I lied.

There was a pea soup fog outside when I walked to the garage with him. When I started up the stairs, he said, "You don't have to come up the rest of the way. I'll be okay."

"I want to see if you're keeping your room neat," I lied.

His room was neat and his closet held nothing but clothes. He was smiling.

"What's funny?" I asked.

"You," he said. "Good night, Uncle Brock."

I rumpled his hair. I went out and waited until I heard him double-lock the door before going down the steps. Jan was putting away her samples and her catalogues.

"Should I make some cocoa?" I asked.

"If there's any milk left. Juan has been on a milk binge lately."

There was plenty of milk. Trust Mrs. Casey to make

sure of that. I added some cinnamon and a touch of cognac.

"Should we watch the eleven o'clock news on the tube?" Jan asked.

"Not tonight," I said.

17

THE GRAY METAL button in the hand of the dead Andropolus seemed to me to be strong ammunition for Nowicki's defense of Ricardo. But Fran was right; it would also alert the killer. Ricardo was a kinsman; Fran had twin goals, to clear Ricardo and punish the man who had framed him. His second goal was probably as compulsive as the first.

We had cut a few corners on the case I had shared with him before. But it hadn't included anything as drastic as withholding evidence.

There was also the doubtful possibility that the button was a ploy, a button ripped from the jacket of an innocent person and put into the dead man's hand, a pointer pointing in the wrong direction.

"You're looking gloomy this morning," Jan said at breakfast.

"I'm pondering the imponderables," I explained.

"What does that mean?" Juan asked.

"It means he's in over his head," Jan told him.

"Like in swimming?"

"More or less," I said.

"You don't have to stay involved in this," Jan pointed out. "You can always quit, Brock."

Juan's face stiffened. "Uncle Brock would *never* quit!"

Jan sighed. "I know."

Juan went to Omega after breakfast, Jan downtown. Uncle Brock went back to pondering the imponderables. Relationships had become clearer, motives revealed and suspicions strengthened. But the only solid piece of evidence we had was a button.

That might be the clincher but not, at the moment, a clue. Toledo, Culver, Kranski, and the unlamented Andropolus had all come here from Los Angeles.

I phoned the sheriff's station and asked McClune if any of those names had been on the lists of the two Los Angeles stores.

He told me they hadn't. "But remember that the only lists they had were those of their charge account customers. They use them for mailing. Thanks for the stuff you gave Fran last night."

"You're welcome. Don't tell Chief Harris about it."

"I don't plan to. If that windbag gives you any static feel free to use my name."

I was discussing the crabgrass in our front lawn with our once-a-week gardener when Mrs. Casey came out to tell me I had a phone call.

It was Sergeant Ethel Wingram, the woman who shared an office with Kranski. She told me, "Karl won't be in until noon. And one of my new probationers told me something about him yesterday that I find difficult to believe. I know you are a friend of his and a former investigator and I'd like to talk with you."

"Why?"

"Because, if what she told me is true, I would be morally bound to report it to Chief Harris."

"I see," I said, though I didn't. "I'll be down there in half an hour."

She had a surprise for me when I entered her office; her formerly dull brown hair was now a garish lemon yellow.

She must have noticed my stare. "Do you like it?" she asked.

I lied with a nod. "It really brightens up the room." I sat in the chair near her desk. "What shenanigans is our friend Kranski involved with now"

"It's more serious than shenanigans," she said. "Have you ever heard of the Elysian Massage Parlor?"

"I know where it is. I suspect they go a little further than therapeutic massage."

"They certainly do! My young probationer formerly worked there."

"Is that why she was busted?"

"No. We could never prove a thing on them. The girl was put on probation for possession of marijuana. It was her first offense. She told me yesterday that Karl quite often frequented the place."

"Recently?"

"Yes. Why did you ask that?"

"I'd rather not say right now."

"I've heard some rumors around here," she said.

"Let's hope they're not true. Was your probationer the girl who served Karl at that place?"

"No. It was an older woman. The only name I have is her first name, Yvette."

"There can't be more than one by that name there. Ethel, whether Karl is guilty or not. I don't think you should tell Chief Harris. He is too strict, most officers claim, on minor transgressions."

"Probably *male* officers," she said scornfully.

"Probably," I agreed. "But they are the chauvinist pigs we have to get along with, aren't they?"

"Yes," she admitted sadly. "You'll keep me informed, won't you?"

"Of course," I promised.

The Elysian Massage Parlor was almost directly across

the street from Rubio's Rendezvous. The sign below the opaque glass of the front door informed me that they were open from two o'clock in the afternoon to two o'clock in the morning.

I walked across the street to Rubio's. He was alone in the place, reading the *Racing Form.*

He looked at me doubtfully. "You've become a morning drinker?"

"Nope. Maybe some coffee. I planned to visit that place across the street but they don't open until two o'clock."

"The whorehouse?"

"Not as a customer! I wanted to question a woman named Yvette. I don't know her last name."

He put a cup of coffee in front of me. "I do. She used to come in here before that place opens and try to pick up some extra dinero. I told her to stay away. Her name is Yvette Apoyan."

"Do you know where she lives?"

"Where she belongs—at the Travis Hotel. Tell me, Pancho, is it true what I heard? Is it hopeless? Do they have a good case against Ricardo?"

"They think they do."

"That's enough for *them,* isn't it?"

"So far," I admitted. "Maybe something will turn up. Maybe Yvette will have something we can use."

He shrugged. "Maybe. But you'll have to pay for it. She doesn't hand out freebies."

San Valdesto is a tourist town and the lodgings range from the Biltmore on the beach down through the better motels and the lesser motels to bed-and-breakfast houses. The Travis does not attract the tourist trade, unless one includes migrants.

I knew the clerk at the desk, a thin, black man in a clean white shirt. He looked at me skeptically.

"It's not what you think," I explained. "I'm working with the police but I'm not here to bust her."

"Room two-eleven," he said. "She ought to be up by now."

There are no elevators in the place. I walked up to the second floor and knocked on the door of 211.

From the other side of the door a feminine voice asked, "Who is it?"

"A friend of Karl Kranski's," I told her.

"You got a name?"

"Karl didn't tell me I needed one. I'm not a cop, Ms. Apoyan."

The door opened and a tall, full figured woman with jet black hair and eyes almost as dark studied me for a moment. She was wearing a yellow satin robe. Her feet were bare, her toenails lacquered a brilliant red.

"I don't usually work mornings," she said. "But any friend of Karl's is a friend of mine. Come in."

I went in. She closed the door behind me. She said, "No kinky stuff. I hope Karl explained that to you."

"I'm not here for that," I said. "I'm investigating the death of a man named Chris Andropolus. Do you know the name?"

She nodded. "They're holding some Mexican for that, aren't they?"

"Ricardo Cortez," I said. "But there are people who have reason to hate Karl and are trying to involve him in it. His niece was married to Andropolus."

"I know."

"Andropolus was killed last Thursday night," I said, and—"

I was interrupted by a knock on her door. Several seconds later the door opened and a fairly short, thin, and swarthy man came into the room.

He didn't look like a local type. He was wearing a big

collared, cream colored silk shirt open almost to his navel. Over it he wore a golden bolero jacket, embroidered in black. His trousers were skin tight and black with bell bottoms.

He glanced at me and glared at Yvette. "Free lancing again, you bitch! I warned you about that, Yvette."

"He's not a customer," she said.

"Don't lie." He looked at me and nodded at the door. "Get out!"

I shook my head. "I haven't finished talking with her."

"Yes, you have. Go!"

I shook my head again.

How he got a switchblade knife out of his pocket in pants as tight as those was a puzzle to me. But suddenly it was there and the blade snicked open.

"Don't do anything foolish," I warned him. "The desk clerk must know you're up here."

He shook his head. "Get out of here!"

"Okay." I started for the door.

And the damned fool began to close his knife! I caught him flush on the mouth with a backhand slap. He stumbled into the wall. I had his wrist in my grip two seconds later and the knife dropped to the floor. He reached down for it, and my knee came up to collide with his chin.

He was on the floor, belly down, and I was holding him there by his neck when the desk clerk appeared in the open doorway.

He looked at the pimp and shook his head. "How the hell did *he* get up here?"

"I don't know. But I think maybe you had better call the law."

He shook his head again. "No need, Mr. Callahan. They'd have to pick up Yvette, too. We'll take care of this. Get up, Andre! It's time for another one of our little talks."

They went out and the door closed behind them. Yvette asked, "Are you Brock Callahan?"

I nodded.

"Karl has mentioned you," she said. "Didn't you play football together?"

"Yes. And now he could be in trouble. Was he with you last Thursday night?"

"The night the Greek was killed?" She paused. "If he wants me to say he was, I will."

"Not unless it's the truth," I warned her. "You could go up for perjury. And then I and the rest of his friends might never nail the real killer."

"He wasn't with me," she said. "Not last Thursday night."

"How about Andre?" I asked. "Do you think he'll be back?'

She shook her head. "He must have come up those side steps the girls on this floor use. He's been warned before. If he has any sense, he'll get out of town."

"Well, thank you for your cooperation."

She smiled. "Any time. I guess I owe you a free one, huh?"

"I smiled back at her. "That would be nice—but my wife would holler at me. She is a *very* jealous woman."

"I don't blame her. Good luck, big boy."

Both the desk clerk and Rubio had voiced it; there are the "we's" and there are the "they's". The "we's" police their own territory and mete out their own brand of justice.

I went to the station from there and Bernie was in. I said, "I understand Harris has decided Ricardo is your man and he's called off the investigation."

"Ricardo is not *my* man! Did you come here to gloat?"

I shook my head. "To take you to lunch. I'm working with the county now."

"Don't tell me McClune supports your vigilante views on proper police procedure."

"It's possible. He came here from Texas. Let's go to lunch and I'll relate the thrilling stories of my recent adventures."

"As long as you're buying," he said, "I'll listen."

At Plotkin's Plaza Cafe I told him all that I had learned since last we talked, except for the button bit, and finished with the semi-comic scene in room 211.

It wasn't comic to him. "The guy had a knife and you don't even carry a gun. You're crazy, man!"

"I have a gun and a permit to carry it," I told him. "Why would I need one against a pimp in a bolero jacket?"

"Oh, God!" he said. "The world changes but you go blithely on in your primitive way. Don't you read the papers?"

"At times. Another martini?"

"Thank you, yes."

When the waiter brought it he took a small sip and put on his professorial look. A lecture was coming.

"You have narrowed your suspects to three. I'm sure the thought never came to you that there might be dozens of others who had a reason to hate Andropolus. The man was a hoodlum, remember, and the enemies of guys like that are legion. At the station we can't pick and choose our cases. There aren't enough officers or hours in a twenty-four-hour day to keep up with the flood. But more man hours have been put in on the Andropolus case than you could investigate in a month. And new cases keep pouring in: rapes, murders, burglaries, child molestation, wife beating, larceny, assault, robberies, arson, terrorists, kooks. The courts are jammed, calendars months behind, and the lackadaisical citizens scream for better police protection."

I smiled at him. "I know all that, Bernie. But I am a non-lackadaisical citizen."

"Yes," he admitted wearily. "And it's the only reason I tolerate you. Let's eat."

We ate and I walked back to the station with him. There he said, "I suppose you'll be working with Fran Sanchez."

"Probably."

"He's the best man they have," he said, "but, not unlike you, he occasionally lets his temper get the best of him. Keep it cool."

"I'll do my best, Lieutenant."

I was getting into my car when Kranski came out of the station. I said, "Hi!"

He stared at me coldly and walked past to his car. I had made another enemy. I waited until he pulled off the lot before starting my car.

He turned left on Main Street, heading for the freeway. But as I drove past the Travis Hotel his car was parked in front. Either Yvette had phoned him about my morning visit or he was hoping for an afternoon session.

I called the county sheriff's station when I came home and asked for Sanchez. He wasn't in. But McClune was and I told him what I had learned.

"Which means," he said, "that Kranski still doesn't have an alibi for Thursday night. Are you going to tell Sergeant Wingram about this Yvette Apoyan?"

"I doubt it. I'm sure there are officers down there who knew about Flora Benedict. I know Vogel does. Let her find out from them. And it wouldn't surprise me if a few in your department occasionally indulge in a little adultery."

"But not murder. If Kranski wasn't married to a Woolrick, Harris would have him under investigation right now."

"Probably," I agreed.

"Well," he said wearily, "if Fran comes up with anything I'll have him phone you. Do you get the feeling we're nowhere?"

"Yes. But I also have the feeling that Ricardo was framed. I'll stay with it."

"Fran will be glad to hear that. Good hunting, Brock."

I added the new character to my cast, Yvette Apoyan. What would that be, a French Armenian? I now had enough characters to stage a big production musical. The only revelation in the file was that Karl Kranski liked to bed down with big women. Though his approach to Sarah Felderstadt indicated he might sample a small one at times.

I was putting the papers away when the phone rang. It was Chief Harris.

"What the hell is going on between you and Kranski?" he asked.

"You'll have to ask him."

"I did. And he said you had been harassing him, that you suspect him of killing Andropolus."

"He lied. Did he tell you about Yvette Apoyan?"

"He did. She's one of his informants. And he explained to me where he was the night Andropolus was killed."

"Did he also explain it to Lois?"

"No. For reasons that are none of your business. I don't like you digging into department affairs, Brock. I've been tolerant with you, but you must remember you have no official status."

"That," I told him, "you will have to clear with Sheriff McClune. If he agrees with you, call me back." I hung up.

Either he didn't phone McClune or he did and McClune set him straight. Either way, he didn't call back.

18

As the phrase goes, Ricardo had been caught red-handed, caught at the scene of the murder of a man he had reason to hate. It would be difficult for Nowicki to sell Ricardo's story of the phone call to a jury against evidence that overwhelming.

If Andropolus had phoned him and suggested a truce, and also added that neither of them had reason to trust the police and he would reveal to Ricardo the names of the men who had shot at him, why had they fought? That would be the question in the jurors' minds.

Nowicki would probably manage to get some Chicanos on the jury, but it would be predominantly gringos. And they *knew,* or thought they did, what hotheads Mexicans are. The DA had a case.

When Juan came home he told me he had hit two doubles and a single today.

"Good," I said.

"You look grumpy." he said. "Are you still pondering the imponderables?"

"I've just quit. Let's go out and play catch."

"Throw me some high ones," he said, "some pop flys. I dropped a couple today, but it was windy out there. That can happen when it's windy, can't it?"

"It sure can. And if you play with the Dodgers you'll have to play the Giants in Candlestick Park and it's *always* windy up there."

"Are the Dodgers the best?"

"Not this year. But they're my favorite team."

"Then they'll be mine," he said.

If I hadn't been a chauvinistic jerk too stubborn to marry a woman who made more money than I did . . .

I underhanded about two dozen sky-high balls and he missed only two. "Enough?" I asked.

"Ten more," he said. "I want to catch them all."

I threw him ten more and he caught every one.

"Five more?" he asked.

That was when the police car pulled into our driveway. Kranski was behind the wheel; Father Murphy in the seat next to him.

"Damn!" Juan said. He started walking toward the garage as Kranski got out of the car.

"Hold it, boy!" Kranski called.

Juan didn't even look around. He kept walking.

"He's going up to take his shower," I said. "What's this all about?"

Father Murphy was out of the car now. "It's about Juan," he explained. "The sergeant has explained to me that you had no legal right to take Juan away from the Shelter."

"Sergeant Kranski," I told him, "is not a lawyer." I looked at him. "What is this, a vendetta, you vindictive bastard?"

"There is no need for that kind of talk," Father Murphy said sternly. "The district attorney agrees with Sergeant Kranski. Juan's father has returned to town and intends to make a home for him."

"His father? You talked with Juan's father?"

He shook his head. "Sergeant Kranski has. Juan's father is staying at the Travis Hotel. You could phone him there."

I smiled at Kranski. "So that's why you stopped in

there this afternoon. I thought you were dropping in on Yvette for a matinee quickie."

Kranski glared at me. Father Murphy asked, "Who is Yvette?"

"One of Sergeant Kranski's horizontal informants," I said. "Let's go into the house. I want to phone my attorney."

"Like hell!" Kranski said. "We came for the kid."

"Gentlemen, please!" Father Murphy said. "This is no time for acrimony. Juan's welfare should be our only concern."

And then, from the open front doorway, Mrs. Casey said, "What's going on out here?"

"They've come for Juan," I said.

"Over my dead body," she said.

Father Murphy sighed and looked at Kranski. "Perhaps we had better go in and talk this over."

Kranski nodded. "He can phone his attorney. I'm calling the DA."

"First," Father Murphy said gently but firmly, "we will talk."

We went into the living room and talked; Mrs. Casey heatedly, I sarcastically, Kranski threateningly, and Father Murphy quietly.

Finally Mrs. Casey suggested, "Before we phone any attorneys, I think it would be only fair to ask Juan how he feels about all this. I'll go get him."

Kranski started to object. Father Murphy held up a warning hand and said, "I think we should."

She left the room and we sat in silence. We sat and sat. About ten minutes later, I said, "I'll go and find out what's happening."

"I'll go along," Kranski said.

We all went out to the garage and up the steps to Juan's room. Neither he nor Mrs. Casey was there.

When we came down again she was waiting for us. "He isn't here. I've been questioning the neighbors," she said. "None of them saw him leave."

Kranski smirked. "I'll bet that *you* did."

She glared at him.

I said, "Karl, if anything happens to that kid I'll come looking for you."

"You won't need to," he said, "I'll be back."

They were getting into the car when I asked Mrs. Casey, "Where did you hide him?"

She shook her head, "So help me, I didn't. That poor, scared boy!"

"He'll be all right," I soothed her.

"He had better be," she said, "or the Bishop will hear about Father Murphy's part in this. I think you should phone the sheriff."

I phoned McClune and told him what had happened. He promised to send out the call. And he assured me that he would phone Chief Harris and explain to him that the next time he sent a city officer into county territory he had damned well better clear it first with the sheriff's department.

When I hung up, Mrs. Casey came in to tell me: "I won't be able to cook tonight. I'm going to my room."

"I understand."

She went to her room. I phoned the Tomorrow Club and Pete was there. I told him what had happened.

"My father's in town?"

"Yes. It's possible that Juan is heading for your place. Is Sarah home?"

"No. I'll go there. I'll tell Orlando to call me if Juan comes here. Do you know where my father is staying?"

"I do. And I'm going down to talk with him."

"You tell him for me that if he tries to grab Juan I'll make him sorry he was born."

"Easy, Pete! Remember he's still your father."

"Why should I remember? *He* never did. This is all Kranski's work."

"Yes. What's your father's first name?"

"Cruz. You can ask Nowicki about him. He jumped bail when Stan was defending him. That's when he left town."

"That could be a plus for us. There might still be a warrant out for him on the bail jumping charge. Go home, Pete," I said. "I'll keep in touch."

At the Travis Hotel, the desk clerk smiled at me. "Well, Mr. Callahan, I didn't expect to see you this soon again. Yvette isn't in, if that's why you're here."

"Not this time. I came to talk with a man named Cruz Chavez. Is he registered here?"

There were two men occupying the wooden chairs that stood in a row facing the big window that looked out on the street. He pointed to the one in the chair next to the potted palm tree.

The man was dozing, his head slumped forward. The odor of cheap wine was strong as I took the chair next to him. He had a long, narrow face, a thin, hooked nose, a gray-streaked moustache, and long, lank gray hair. He opened his eyes as I sat down.

"Mr. Chavez," I said, "your son Juan has been living with me. I understand you have come back to make a home for him."

He studied me for a few seconds and then nodded.

"Do you have a job?"

He nodded again and closed his eyes.

"Is it a night job?" I asked.

There was no answer from him; he was asleep again. The clerk was smiling again when I got up. I went over there.

"When did he check in?" I asked.

"Two days ago."

"And Kranski talked with him this afternoon?"

"Mr. Callahan, please! I don't want no trouble with the law."

"Nor with me, either, I'm sure."

He sighed. He said, "Kranski talked with him this afternoon and paid his rent a week in advance. Remember now, you didn't hear it from me."

"I didn't. Thank you." I put a ten dollar bill on the desk and walked the two blocks to Nowicki's office. He was there.

After I had finished giving him the sordid history of the last two hours he told me that Pete had phoned and told him most of it. "I phoned Chief Harris and reminded him that Cruz Chavez had jumped bail. He said they had quashed the warrant. And then he reminded me that Pete had violated his probation. What the hell is this supposed to be, a trade-off?"

"It's closer to revenge. We're dead, huh?"

"Not completely. Cruz started wandering years ago. I called Sheriff McClune and he's going to check for any possible warrants out on him from other towns."

"Stan, isn't that a violation of the attorney-client relationship?"

"Not on this one," he said. "Not since that bastard jumped bail. *I* put up the bail."

My stomach was rumbling when I got back to the car, my ulcer burning. I sat for a while before starting the engine and heading for home.

Jan was out in back, sitting in a deck chair. She said, "Mrs. Casey told me what happened. I gave her some valium. She's resting now. Anything new?"

I told her what I had learned downtown.

"And now we sit and wait?" she asked.

I nodded.

"I think we should have a drink," she said.

"I'll make you one, but I'll settle for baking soda and water. Gin, vodka, whiskey, beer?"

"Bourbon over ice."

The baking soda helped a little. Jan took a sip of her drink and said, "If Juan's father goes into court looking and acting the way you described him, wouldn't the judge realize he's not a fit father?"

"Probably. I'm not worried about that or Father Murphy's Shelter. I'm worried about where Juan is and Kranski's next move. As Harris told Nowicki, Pete is still guilty of that parole violation."

"Would it help if I phoned Lois and suggested a truce?"

I shook my head. "She lives in her own world and Kranski in the real one. He doesn't want a truce and there is nothing you can tell her about him that she'd believe."

She nodded agreement and took a deep breath. "I suppose we ought to eat *something.*"

"Later. Maybe a bowl of soup and a sandwich?"

"Later," she agreed.

We had finished our tomato soup and were about to start on the sandwiches when Pete phoned. "Juan's here," he said.

"Thank God! How did he get there?"

"He walked! He stayed away from the busy streets. Jesus, that's a nine mile hike! He's taking a nap now."

"Keep him hidden. We're still not out of the woods. Let him stay there tonight and bring him here tomorrow night. Can you stay home from work?"

"Sure. Did you talk with my father?"

"I tried to, but he kept falling asleep. I guess he'd had too much wine."

"Damn him! Okay, tomorrow night."

I phoned the sheriff's department to tell them that Juan had been found, and came back to the table and told Jan. I said, "Pete's bringing him here tomorrow night. I'll be working tomorrow and I don't want him here until I come home."

"Why don't you give Mrs. Casey that big pistol you used to carry in Los Angeles? Then Pete can bring Juan home tonight," she said bitterly.

She didn't mean it. I recognized her frustration. I felt the same way myself.

"I'm going to miss him, Brock," she said.

"So am I. But I have you and you have me. Let's settle for that."

She nodded. "I'll wake Mrs. Casey and tell her Juan's all right."

She went up to give Mrs. Casey the news. And then, though it was far short of our usual bedtime, we went to bed. A half hour of tossing and turning later we decided on a mutual physical catharsis.

The morning was foggy. Jan waited until it cleared before going to work. The sun was out and blazing when Fran phoned with more good news. The Oxnard police department had a warrant out for Cruz Chavez. He had been living with (and probably off) a waitress in their town who was trying to bring up three young kids.

"Is there a law in Oxnard against that?"

"Not that I know of. The charge is child molestation. McClune has already notified Chief Harris. I have a feeling Pete's probation violation will not be brought up again."

"That's for sure."

"I think," Fran went on, "we've been giving too much attention to our favorite suspects. That Andre Martin you ran into yesterday is tied up with the best organized gringo gang in town."

"It's hard to believe he could have killed Andropolus."

"That's true. But it was the corner of the desk that killed Andropolus. Chris could have stumbled into it going after Andre."

"Fran!"

"Crazy," he admitted. "But what else do we have?'

"Nothing," I agreed.

It was probably no crazier than my current Kranski obsession. If Karl had been a Ram, I wondered, would I have been less suspicious of him?

I phoned Pete and told him about Fran's call. I said, "I guess the heat is off. You can bring Juan over this morning if you want to. That way you won't miss a whole day at work."

Pete said, "He's been moaning all morning about missing baseball practice. He said if I would drive him out there, the coach would bring him home."

"Okay. Tell him we miss him."

"So do we."

Lois Kranski had told me that Shirley had suspected Chris of adultery. If he had been involved with a married woman there could be a jealous husband out there in the vast unsuspected.

When I had talked with Shirley outside her house that day I was trying to find Peter Chavez, she had expressed the hope that I would be successful. It seemed reasonable to expect that she would be even more eager to have her husband's killer found.

I drove up the long winding road to the lannon stone

and stucco house at the top of the rise. I stood on the parking area for a moment, soaking in the view of the morning sun on the pastoral Santa Ynez Valley to the north.

I turned toward the house just as the front door opened. Shirley Andropolus was again wearing designer jeans, but her turtleneck sweater was yellow today, not light blue, and her right eye no longer discolored.

"You again?" she asked.

I nodded. "Do you remember me?"

"I do. And Lois Kranski has told me about you since then. What is it this time?"

"I'm back on the hunt," I explained. "Last time it was a boy. This time I hope to find the person who had a fight with your husband."

"You don't think it was Ricardo Cortez?"

"I'm not sure what I think any more. I've been lied to by too many people."

"So have I," she said. "Would you like a cup of coffee?"

I nodded.

"Follow me," she said.

I followed her to the kitchen, about halfway down the long hallway that divided the house. It was an immense farm kitchen, except for the modern accessories. They included a built-in charcoal grill, an espresso machine, a drip coffee maker, a microwave oven, and four chrome and plastic upholstered chairs around a chrome legged and hard plastic topped table. I sat in one of the chairs.

"Maybe a Danish?" she asked.

"Why not?"

She took two rolls out of the freezer and put them into the microwave oven. She poured me a cup of coffee and asked, "Why should you be concerned with who killed my husband? You weren't exactly friends."

"That's true. Mostly, I guess, it's because I feel there is a strong possibility that Ricardo isn't guilty."

"Is *he* a friend of yours?"

"Not really."

She brought the pastry to the table, sat down across from me, and asked, "What are you—one of those indignant citizens?"

"At times. Is that bad?"

She shrugged. "I guess not. Mr. Callahan, I have no idea who killed Chris."

I took a chance and said, "It could have been a jealous husband."

She stiffened and glared at me. "Who told you about that?"

"Does it matter?"

"Lois," she guessed.

I said nothing.

She took a bite of her pastry and a sip of coffee. She said quietly, "My husband was unfaithful to me. But I don't know who the woman was, so I wouldn't know if she was married."

"Your husband admitted it?"

She shook her head. "I hired a private detective."

"And he never found out who the woman was?"

"I don't know. To tell you the truth, I didn't give a damn. I had already learned more than I wanted to know."

"Was he a local investigator?"

She nodded. "But if I tell you his name he could be in trouble, couldn't he—for withholding evidence? At least, that's what he told me."

"He could be. But he won't. At the moment I am also

withholding evidence. We private investigators don't always work within the strict letter of the law."

She took another sip of coffee and stared at me. Finally she said,"His name is Wendell Packard. His office is in the Woggon Building."

19

THE WOGGON BUILDING was an ancient four-story, yellow brick building in the older section of the business district. I went up in the creaky elevator. It stopped about six inches below the fourth floor.

The office of Wendell Packard was at the rear of the building. The lettering on the opaque glass of his door revealed that he dealt in bail bonds, credit investigations, missing persons, process serving, and workmen's compensation. It did not mention adultery.

It was a one-man, one-room, two-chair, one-desk office. The man sitting behind the desk was gray-haired and thin, about sixty. He was wearing a blue serge jacket. He stood up as I came in and I saw that his trousers matched his jacket. His bow tie was a blue on white polka dot.

"Mr. Packard?" I asked.

He nodded.

"My name is Brock Callahan."

"I've heard of you," he said. "Be seated, Mr. Callahan."

I sat in the chair next to his desk. "I've just come from a talk with Shirley Andropolus. She told me you did some work for her."

He nodded again. "And—?"

"I wondered if you learned the name of the woman her husband was involved with."

He shook his head. "No. And about the rest of it—

with Andropolus murdered, you must understand my position."

"Withholding evidence?" I smiled at him. "So am I. And, just between us, so is Sheriff McClune. I'm working with his department. You can phone him to confirm that, if you want to."

"No need. I never learned the name of the woman."

"You didn't follow her home?"

"No. I was following Andropolus. The woman was waiting for him in front of the motel when I got there. That was around seven o'clock in the evening. I sat in front until two o'clock, waiting for them to come out. I am not a young man, as you may have noticed. I need my sleep. And I already had enough to confirm what Mrs. Andropolus suspected."

"Did you get a good look at the woman?"

He shook his head again. "Only from a distance. She was tall and slim. Her hair was black, straight and short, with bangs."

"You didn't check with the desk clerk?"

"Mr. Callahan! You can't be serious! Are you assuming they'd use their right names? And what authority would I have to interrogate the clerk?"

"It was a dumb question," I admitted. "What night was that?"

He reached into a file drawer in his desk and took out a folder of papers. He ruffled through them and said, "It was Monday night, June seventeenth, at the Ridge Motel." He put the file back into the drawer. "And that, sir, is all the information I have."

I thanked him and went out. I stood in front of the elevator door, listening to it creak and groan from below, and decided one show of bravado was enough for one day. I walked down the four flights of stairs.

I used the wall phone in the lobby to phone McClune.

I told him what I had learned, attributing it all to Shirley Andropolus and not mentioning Packard. I explained that I didn't have the authority to interrogate the clerk and that if he was the night clerk he wouldn't be on duty now.

"The registration cards will be there," he said. "Fran will meet you there in half an hour."

The Ridge Motel was on a bluff overlooking the ocean, the largest and most expensive motel in town. The rooms facing the ocean cantilevered out from the bluff, a hundred feet of nothing but air between them and the rocky beach below. And this was earthquake country.

I was listening to a Glenn Miller golden oldie from a Los Angeles radio station that featured the big band era when Fran drove into the parking lot.

As we walked to the doorway he said, "This place has a reputation of catering to the local hot pillow trade. But how much of that will they admit? Hell, all hotels and motels accept unmarried couples today."

"Adultery is not our concern, Fran. It's murder."

The clerk referred us to the manager. He was in his office, a short, balding, penguin-shaped man wearing what was probably a permanent look of harassment.

Fran identified himself and explained why we were there.

The man sighed. "I hope we are not going to get any unfavorable publicity out of this."

"There's no reason why you should," Fran assured him. "All we need to see are the registration cards for the seventeenth of June."

He went into a small room behind the office and brought out about two dozen registration cards. They all included the hour of registration; there were only three couples who had registered around seven o'clock.

Fran asked, "Do you recognize these names?"

The man read them and shook his head. "I don't work nights." He paused and then said, "June seventeenth—the man at the desk was working nights that week. Perhaps he might remember them."

The clerk at the desk remembered one couple. They were fairly frequent guests, he told us, a Mr. and Mrs. Christian Greco. The husband was short and bulky, with a crew haircut and a slight scar below his right eye. He always wore dark glasses.

"Did he pay by credit card?" Fran asked.

The clerk smiled and shook his head. "Never."

"Do you remember the woman?"

He smiled again. He obviously did not share the manager's peevishness. "Oh, yes, a very elegant lady, slim and tall, with one of those Colleen Moore haircuts."

"Colleen Moore?" Fran asked. "Who in hell is she?"

"An ancient movie star," I told him, "with short hair and bangs, now dead."

The clerk looked at me admiringly. "A fellow addict! Have you ever wondered if this Ricardo Cortez the police are holding is related to the original?"

I nodded.

"Could we get back to the here and now?" Fran asked acidly. "Is there any more information you can give us on the couple?"

"Well—they spent all their time in the room."

"Would you be able to identify the woman if you saw her again?"

"Until my dying day," the clerk told him.

Outside, Fran said, "That guy is really weird, huh?"

"Most ancient movie buffs are. He described Andropolus well, though, didn't he?"

"Yes. Jesus, Christian Greco—! And wearing sunglasses at night. He and that clerk could start their own kook club."

"Don't tell me you don't remember Ricardo Cortez."
"Of course I do! But Colleen Moore?"
"To each his own, Fran. We Anglos remember her."
He shook his head. "Ricardo's about to get railroaded and we're quibbling about old movie stars. And Harris covering for Kranski. Where the hell are we?"
"One suspect closer than we were yesterday. And I can't believe Chandler Harris would cover for Kranski if he had any reason to suspect he was guilty. He's still cop enough to demand proof."
Fran shrugged. "Maybe. Well, I'm heading for a little talk with that pimp, Andre. How about you?"
"If I knew where to start I'd go hunting for the woman Andropolus was with."
"There are two people who might know about her," Fran said. "Tony Toledo and George Culver. But it's a cinch that neither of those two would confide in the law."
"I get the message. I'm elected."
He nodded and smiled. "Good luck, peeper."
Both Toledo and Culver had been Andropolus's associates. It was not likely that sentimental loyalty would be one of their virtues. But, then again, it might be.
I drove down to the office of Abbot and Clarke.
Tony was in his cubicle, talking on the phone. I waited until he had finished before entering.
He smiled at me. "Now might be a good time to buy some more of that Amicor International. It's gone down seven points in the last three days."
"I came to question, not to buy," I said. I told him what I had learned at the Ridge Motel.
"So?" he said. "Now, what's the question?"
"I wondered if you might know who the woman was."
He shook his head. "I don't. Believe it or not, Chris

had a way with women. It couldn't have been his looks. It must have been his money—or his dong."

"If she was married and had a jealous husband, maybe Ricardo isn't the man we want."

His face hardened. He stared at me. "And I'm a jealous husband—is that what you're saying?"

"No. This woman had black hair. But I thought as you were a friend of his, you might be concerned with who killed him and would want the guilty man punished."

"Sure I do."

"And now that you've become a solid citizen, I thought maybe you could ask around among your former associates."

He shook his head. "They no longer confide in me. Culver would be your best bet."

"I doubt if he'd talk to me."

"I think he would if you tell him what you learned this morning. I'm sure he thought enough of Chris to want his killer put away."

I said nothing.

He leaned back in his chair. "Aren't you tilting at windmills, Callahan? The DA has a solid case. I've dropped Kranski from my favored suspect list. Cortez is the odds-on bet. That story he fed the sheriff has more holes than a sieve."

"It has," I agreed. "What I can't believe is that Ricardo would be dumb enough to use it—unless it was true."

"Maybe he's dumber than you think." He smiled. "Do you want me to put in an order for some more Amicor International?"

"Not here," I said. "I've switched my account to Charles Schwab."

That took the smile off his face.

I didn't look forward to meeting George Culver again. But I had no place else to go. I saw Lois Kranski's ancient Mercedes on the Andropolus parking area as I went past.

A light green Cadillac was parked by Culver's house when I drove up his long, winding driveway. I sat in the car for a few minutes, doubting that I would be welcome, trying to frame a persuasive opening approach.

I had to ring twice before the door opened. "Jesus," he said, "*you*! Now what?"

I said, "Tony Toledo suggested that I come here. I have some information he thought you might want to know."

"About what?"

"About the death of your friend Andropolus."

He took a deep breath and stared at me skeptically. Finally, he said, "Come in."

I followed him back to his small office and took the chair I had sat in before. He sat behind his desk and said, "Okay, start talking."

I related most of what I had learned this morning, from my talk with Shirley Andropolus to Toledo's suggestion that I come here. I did not include the name of Wendell Packard.

I said, "We're on opposite sides of the fence. But I figured you would be just as concerned about who killed Chris as I am to clear Cortez."

"You don't know who the woman is?"

I shook my head. "I thought you might."

He was silent for seconds. Finally, "I had a feeling Shirley was worried about Chris. It's not the first time. He was a real quiff hound. The damned fool even got involved with the wife of a police lieutenant in L.A. Shirley never learned about that. And I never heard about this latest one. Do you have a description of her?"

"Only that she is a tall, slim brunette, that's all. Chris signed the register as Mr. and Mrs. Christian Greco."

"That flake! But you're right. He was my friend. You learn anything more, let me know. I'll make it worth your while."

"I don't work for pay these days," I told him. "Whatever I learn goes to the police."

"Ain't you the fuckin' saint? I checked your history down in L.A., Callahan."

"And I know your Los Angeles rap sheet. Compared with that, I could qualify as a saint."

He smiled at me, one of those phony, happy warrior smiles. "And tough, I heard. Did I hear right?"

I smiled back at him. "Why don't we go outside and find out?"

"Not today," he said. "My arthritis is acting up. Maybe later. Thanks for the info, peeper. I'll put my boys to work on it."

I went out and down the road toward home. Mrs. Kranski's Mercedes was no longer in front of the Andropolus house. If I hurried, I could have lunch with Mrs. Casey. I hurried.

20

A PRE-LUNCH DRINK and a ham and cheese omelette later, Mrs. Casey went up to her afternoon soporifics and I back to the tangle of names, possible motives, and doubtful alibis in my record.

The Chicano war had simmered down into an adultery investigation. Andropolus was dead, Toledo had deserted the organization, the chop shop was out of business, Peter Chavez was reunited with his brother. That much had been accomplished.

But Ricardo was still being held. Culver had said he would put his boys to work on it. If they learned anything they certainly would not share it with the police. They had their own brand of justice. Ricardo would still be held; the guilty party dead for reasons unknown to the police.

The "boys" Culver had mentioned could be the same men who had shot at Ricardo. This time they might not be shooting from a moving car.

Fran dispelled that scenario when he came to the house a half hour later. He had just come from his little talk with Andre Martin. Andre had told him that the men who had shot at Ricardo had been out-of-towners, imported by Andropolus.

"They sure as hell couldn't have been pros," I said.

"That figures. The only pros Andropolus seems to

have brought to town are those so-called mechanics he had in the chop shop."

"Did Andre know their names?"

"No. And he told me they had now left town."

"He could be lying about all of it. How would he know who Andropolus had hired?"

He agreed with a nod. "I had the same thought on the way over here. It could have been a couple of his gringo teammates. I'll get to some of the others. Did you talk with Toledo?"

"Yes. And Culver, too." I repeated as accurately as I could remember my dialogues with both of them.

"And Culver is going to send his hoodlums out on the hunt? I think we had better call Chief Harris and alert him."

"Considering the McClune-Harris relationship, I think our best bet is alerting Bernie Vogel. If he's not in the office when I call, I'll call him at home tonight."

"And I'll alert McClune." He took a deep breath. "I hate to say it, but I'm going to. It's really stretching the long arm of coincidence, isn't it, to believe that Ricardo is innocent? If Andropolus actually phoned him, the killer would have had to know about it before Ricardo got there. And if the same person made the phone call to us it would have taken some intricate timing to make sure we got there when Ricardo did."

"It's hard to believe," I agreed. "And it's almost as hard to believe that Andropolus would suggest a truce. I can't read him as that sensible a man. But, as I told Toledo, Ricardo would be dumber than I think he is to come up with a story that strange unless it was the truth."

He sighed. "Again, I hate to say it, but Ricardo is not very bright. And I have reason to know that he's belligerent."

"So have I. Are you quitting, Fran?"

He shook his head stubbornly. "Not yet. Are you?"

"Not yet," I said.

He left and I phoned the station and Bernie was there. I told him about my talk with Culver and said, "I thought I'd better alert you."

"I'm no longer on the case," he said. "You'd better call Chief Harris."

"Bernie—!"

"Okay, I'll tell him. Are you and Fran still on that wild goose chase?"

"Yes. Shouldn't we be?"

There was a silence before he said, "You should. Pardon my cynical remark. It's been a tiring day. I tend to agree with you—Cortez couldn't have come up with a story that kooky unless it was true. Good luck, buddy."

Juan came home with the good news that he had not missed any fly balls today and had hit two doubles in five times at bat. Jan came home with the good news that she would be honored in July as Decorator of the Year at the San Valdesto County Decorator's Convention.

I congratulated both of them and regretted that I had no good news of my own to report.

I was still thinking of Bernie's and Fran's agreement about the absurdity of Ricardo's story when the obvious, which must have been stirring in my usually dependable unconscious, finally came to the surface.

Captain Walsh was running the night watch at the station and we were only lukewarm friends. But I phoned him after dinner and asked if I could come down and talk with Ricardo.

"Ouch!" he said. "With you and the chief feuding as you are? That's asking a lot, Brock."

"It is," I agreed. "Would he have to know about it?"

"I guess not. Would it be a long talk?"
"Three questions at the most."
"Okay," he said.

Ricardo looked thinner. He was sitting on his cot, staring at the floor, when the turnkey let me in.
He looked up and managed a small smile.
I asked him, "Ricardo, are you sure it was Andropolus who phoned you last Thursday night?"
He frowned. "He said it was."
"Have you ever talked with him before?"
He shook his head. "Never. Do you think it was somebody else?"
"I do. Think back, Ricardo. Did it sound like any voice you might have heard before?"
He shook his head. "None. Why?"
"Because I think you were framed. Fran Sanchez agrees with me. We're working together. Keep the faith, Ricardo."
He nodded. "That's all I have left." He smiled again. "Except for you and Francesco."
City cops and county cops and your humble narrator had plodded around asking questions. And not one of us had asked the obvious question—"Are you sure it was Andropolus who phoned you?"
That should have been Nowicki's first question. I called him when I got home, told him what I had learned, and asked him why he hadn't asked the big question.
"God only knows," he said. "I guess I'm dumb. I'll sure as hell bring it up in court. It gives that story of his some substance."
Finding the real killer would give it more substance, I thought, but didn't voice it. All I had was a hunch. It would take more than that to build a case.
Private investigator Wendell Packard, my notes re-

minded me, had sat out in front of the Ridge Motel until two o'clock in the morning. That meant the lovers had most probably spent the night there. They were not afternoon adulterers. That would indicate, if the woman was married, that her husband was out of town. Had Shirley Andropolus also been out of town?

I was still making the connections, trying to establish the pattern, when Jan came to tell me our bedtime cocoa was ready.

We drank it in the kitchen. "You don't look as gloomy as you did when I came home," she said. "Good news?"

"A small ray of light, that's all."

"Do you want to tell me about it?"

I shook my head.

"I'm glad," she said. "Because I don't want to hear about it."

It took me a long time to get to sleep that night, charting my itinerary for tomorrow. I decided my first stop would be the Ridge Motel.

Juan told us at breakfast that there was no practice session or game today. So Mrs. Casey was going to take him to the Museum of Natural History and the Botanic Garden. They would have their lunch downtown.

"And I'll be having my lunch in Solvang," Jan said, and smiled at me. "Don't go overboard at MacDonald's, lover."

I didn't dignify her comment with a reply.

They both left the house before I did. I had some planning to do, having more important things than lunch on my mind.

There was a line waiting to be registered when I arrived at the Ridge Motel—a convention group, complete with identifying badges. It was half an hour later before the clerk had time for me.

"My fellow addict!" he said. "It's refreshing to see a familiar face. What is it this time?"

I told him what I wanted, the registration records of Mr. and Mrs. Christian Greco previous to the seventeenth of June.

He went to the small room behind the manager's office and came back with four registration cards, the earliest a Friday in early May. I copied all the dates.

"Is it the lady who is in trouble," he asked me, "or the gentleman?"

"The gentleman is dead," I told him. "I don't know about the lady, not yet."

He sighed. "I hope she's not in trouble."

I phoned the Andropolus house from there and Shirley answered. I asked her if it would be possible for me to talk with her this morning.

"Why not?" she said. "But no breakfast this time. I have an appointment to have my hair done in an hour."

She was waiting out in front when I got there twenty minutes later. "I hope this won't take long," she said.

"Just a few simple questions. I know that you were out of town last week but I wondered how many times you've been out of town since early May and if you remembered the dates?"

She stared at me suspiciously. "What's this all about?"

"About the death of your husband. If I take time to explain it all, you'll be late for your appointment."

"Last week," she told me, "was the first time I was out of town since Easter week. Chris is the one who took the trips. He said they were business trips."

"You don't think they were?"

"Not any more," she said. "And I'm sure you know why. Is that what you're thinking—that Chris was killed by a jealous husband?"

"It's possible."

"I don't suppose you'd want to tell me his name?"

"I don't have a name yet," I explained, "because I don't know the name of the woman. That detective you hired never learned it. She was a tall, slim woman with a page boy haircut, a brunette. That's all the description he had. But the desk clerk at the Ridge Motel told me he could identify her—if I find her."

"He saw her *once* and he thinks he can still remember her?"

"He saw her more than once," I said. "She was there with Chris five times since early in May."

"That bastard!" she said. "That horny bastard! Uncle Karl was right about him. I have to go now."

Uncle Karl was right. . . . It takes one to know one.

It hadn't been the deceived wife who had been out of town; it had been the adulterous husband. And how about the woman known as Mrs. Christian Greco? Was she married to a traveling salesman? Maybe she wasn't married. If she wasn't married the jealous husband theory would go right down the drain.

It hit me then, what should have hit me before. It was probably Shirley's trip to the beauty parlor that triggered it. I headed for the office of Abbot and Clarke.

Dapper Tony Toledo was alone in his office. He smiled as I came in. "I hope you're here to tell me you've left Charles Schwab."

"Nope." I laid the slip of dates on his desk. "I wondered if you had been out of town on those nights."

He glanced at the slips and stared at me. "Are you playing cop again? What's this all about?"

"Those are the nights Chris Andropolus was sleeping with the woman at the Ridge Motel."

"So what's that got to do with me being out of town?"

"I have this theory that Chris Andropolus might have

sent you out of town on business the same nights he told Shirley he was going out of town on business."

"Damn you!" he said. "Are you suggesting that my wife—" He took a deep breath. "You told me yesterday that the woman had dark hair."

"I know. But it occurred to me about fifteen minutes ago that she might have been wearing a wig."

He was trembling now, but his voice was low and even. "I don't know why you're on this vendetta, Callahan, but I'm not telling you a goddamned thing. I'm going to phone my attorney now and I would like to do it in private. If you think you have a case, I suggest you take it to the police."

"That's where I'm going," I told him.

21

BERNIE WAS IN his office elbow deep in paper work. "I can give you ten minutes," he said curtly.

I told him the story of my morning from the Ridge Motel clerk to Toledo's dismissal.

"Now what do you want from me?" he asked. "A critique?"

"Something a little more substantial than that. I was thinking you could have a talk with Mrs. Toledo. She lives in the city."

"The Ridge Motel is also in the city," he pointed out. "You didn't need me there."

"We could go to lunch and talk it over," I suggested. "The lunch would be on me."

"I brought my lunch," he said. "Brock, the chief told me I was off the case. If you want me to, I'll phone Mrs. Toledo and tell her you're working with us. Do you have her phone number?"

"I don't have it with me. It's an unlisted number. Stan Nowicki knows it."

He pointed to the phone. "Call him."

I phoned him. The volunteer secretary in his office told me he was in court. Could she be of any help?

I told her who I was and what I wanted. She gave it to me. I wrote it down for my own information and read it to Bernie.

He sighed and dialed the number. "Mrs. Toledo?" he asked.

A minute or so later he put the phone back in its cradle and said, "Mrs. Toledo is not home. That was the maid. She said Mrs. Toledo should be home before one o'clock. She's having guests for lunch."

"Thanks, Bernie," I said.

"Don't you want me to call later?"

I shook my head. "I don't need you any more right now. Give my best to the chief."

Back to the Ridge Motel. The manager was behind the desk. The clerk, he told me, was in his office, eating his lunch. Another brown bagger.

"A stakeout?" the clerk said. "I'd like that. When?"

"Now. Bring your lunch. We want to get there before she gets home."

He put his half-eaten sandwich on top of the others in the bag and picked up his vacuum bottle of coffee. He told the manager he might be a few minutes late, but this was official business.

As he climbed into my Mustang he said, "I had a hunch you'd be driving a classic. A sixty-five or a sixty-six?"

"A sixty-six."

It was only a three minute ride to the Toledo house. I drove past, made a U-turn, and parked across the street.

"Could you eat a sandwich?" he asked. "My wife always packs too many. I guess she wants me to get as fat as she is."

"Thanks. I could use one."

"Corned beef or salami?"

"Whatever you don't like."

"You're the guest."

"Corned beef," I decided.

Five minutes later a sleek Camaro came down the

street and turned into the Toledo driveway. The tall, slim, blonde Mavis Toledo got out of it and stared across the street at us.

"That's her," the clerk said. "I know that face. Gad, she's even prettier as a blonde. Who does she remind you of?"

"Veronica Lake. But Veronica was shorter."

"And not as skinny," he added. "She died in nineteen-seventy-three."

"I know. If you have to, would you testify in court that she is the woman who spent her nights with Christian Greco?"

"If I have to, I suppose I would. But I wouldn't like it."

"Just between us," I told him, "the man you had registered as Christian Greco was Chris Andropolus."

"Jesus!" he said. "That hoodlum who was murdered?"

"One and the same."

He chuckled. "You know, I used to think he might be Telly Savalas and *he* was wearing the wig. I'm goofy, huh?"

"We both are," I consoled him. "I'll do my damnedest to keep you out of court."

I dropped him off at the motel and went back to see Vogel. He was eating his lunch. I told him what I had learned and suggested that he could pass it on to the chief. "Tell him it would take the heat off of Kranski."

"The heat is already off Kranski, according to Harris. What you have is proof of adultery on her, but not on Andropolus—yet."

"Plus grounds for a suspicion of murder."

"Only if you can prove the man was Andropolus and Toledo learned what was going on. You want a sandwich?"

"I had one. I helped the desk clerk eat his lunch. So, okay, do what you want. I know you're overworked."

"Don't sulk," he said. "I'll stop in and talk with the Toledos on my way home tonight."

"You are a true public servant," I said.

"Go!" he said.

Bernie was right; all I had was proof of adultery on Mavis Toledo, and not even that on Andropolus. If we could prove that the dates both Toledo and Andropolus were out of town matched up, that might help to strengthen the jealous husband theory. But no jury would accept it as convincing evidence of murder.

I phoned the sheriff's department when I came home. Fran was not there; I told McClune what I had learned from Ricardo the night before and the desk clerk at noon.

"We really blew it, didn't we?" he said. "That makes Ricardo's story more legitimate. Have you talked with Toledo?"

"This morning in his office. He told me to get lost. That was before the clerk confirmed my suspicion. Bernie Vogel told me he would drop in and talk with the Toledos on his way home."

"And Harris agreed?"

"Bernie probably won't tell him. Harris is only his boss. I'm his friend."

"I wish to hell he was running that department. I'll phone him and ask him to meet you and Fran at your house after he talks with Toledo."

Mrs. Casey and Juan were still on their culture trip. I went into her kitchen and made myself a ham and cheese sandwich on sourdough rye bread. I took it and a bottle of Einlicher with me while I went over my notes.

Though he fit the physical description and almost confirmed it with that dumb pseudonym, Andropolus was now ashes. There was no way the desk clerk could identify him.

I was playing catch with Juan when Bernie came. Bernie and I went into the house; Juan stayed outside, bouncing a tennis ball against the garage door.

Over a glass of his favorite Scotch Bernie told me, "I stopped in at the Toledos. It was a short visit. I don't know if Mrs. Toledo was home. She never showed. Toledo's attorney was there. He spoke rather acidly of harassment. I told him we had a positive identification of Mrs. Toledo at the motel and it would be unwise for a so-called officer of the court to be guilty of trying to impede a murder investigation."

"I hope you didn't mention the clerk."

"I didn't. We may have to if push comes to shove."

Fran arrived a few minutes later. He echoed McClune's words: "We sure blew it, didn't we?"

"And we're still a long way from home," I said.

"Hell, yes!" He looked at Bernie. "Did you talk with Mrs. Toledo?"

Bernie shook his head and told him what he had told me. He pointed out that even if Mavis Toledo admitted the man was Andropolus, it didn't automatically prove her husband was guilty.

"He beat up a Hollywood stunt man when he was living in Los Angeles because he suspected him of messing with Mavis," I said.

"That could be a plus but certainly not a clincher," Vogel said.

"My theory," Fran said, "for what it's worth, is that the man who phoned us is the same man who phoned Ricardo. Now, if it had been a nine-eleven emergency call we'd have the caller's phone number. But he called direct."

"I'm not following you," I said.

The way he explained it, the sheriff's department had recently installed a new recording system for 911 emergency calls. It not only recorded the calls, it traced the phone number of the caller before the officer accepted the call. That way, if the caller couldn't finish, the police would know where to go.

"But even if you can't trace the direct calls," Bernie asked, "don't you record them?"

Fran nodded. "We've been doing that for over a year."

Bernie sighed. "So, at least we've got a voice. I'm going to have a talk with Toledo's attorney tomorrow."

"Tomorrow is Saturday," I said. "Are you putting in overtime?"

He nodded. "You guys need me on this one."

They left and I went out to play catch with Juan again. "Those two men were cops, weren't they?" he said.

I nodded. "How could you tell?"

He shrugged. "Is Mr. Cortez still in trouble?"

"Those two cops and I are trying to get him out of it."

"Is that tall cop Italian?"

"His name is Francesco Sanchez. Is that Italian? What are you trying to tell me, Juan?"

He shrugged again.

I said, "The other cop is a Jew and I'm an Irishman. Is it time for another lecture?"

"Let's play catch," he said.

"Not until you answer my question."

"It's not time for another lecture," he said. "I still remember the first one."

He was out in back, reading, when Jan came home with the news that Lois Kranski had taken her to lunch.

"In Solvang?"

"I didn't go to Solvang. The client phoned before I

left the shop and canceled the appointment. Lois asked me to give you a message."

"Why couldn't she call me directly? Has their phone been disconnected?"

"She said she was embarrassed. She wouldn't tell me what it was about. She simply told me to tell you that she was wrong about Karl. What does that mean?"

"It means that the old rich live in their own insular world."

"Could you be a little more explicit?"

"Sorry. It's privileged information. Shall I make you a drink, sweetheart?"

"You may."

We finished our drinks and had dinner and went back to the routine; Juan to the old-movie tube with Mrs. Casey, Jan to the PBS channel, and I to my pondering.

Voice, voice, voice; that had been our blind spot and might now be our salvation. But how could we use it? Let me count the ways . . .

22

JAN WENT TO work in the morning. Pete Chavez came to pick up Juan for the weekend. He told me he hadn't been able to learn anything that could help clear Ricardo.

"But we're still working on it," he said.

"So am I. So are Sheriff McClune, Bernie Vogel, and Fran Sanchez."

He smiled. "But not Chief Harris, I'll bet, or Sergeant Kranski."

"Not them. Who needs 'em? How is Orlando treating you?"

"As well as he can afford. Sarah and I are putting away what we can. I want to get my own garage."

"When the time comes that you're ready, let me know. I have a few loose dollars."

"You're doing enough now," he said. "I'm not looking for any more charity, Mr. Callahan."

"I'm not offering it," I assured him. "It will be a loan at the prevailing interest rate. Plus, of course, the same deal I have at Orlando's shop—I pay for parts only."

"Fair enough. And you'll get the parts at my cost."

When the time came, I would have the best mechanic in town at a price below the worst. And Jan thinks I don't have any economic sense.

The mist that had been drifting in from the ocean was starting to clear when Bernie phoned. He had talked with Toledo's attorney, he told me, and got nowhere.

Mavis had left the house for parts unknown; Toledo was being uncooperative even with his own attorney.

"But," he went on, "McClune and Fran think they have come up with a bright idea. Do you know what a voice oscilloscope is?"

"No."

"Neither do I. Whatever it is, they have one. Fran claims it's almost as infallible as fingerprints."

"Is it admissible in court?"

"We'll ask them that when we get there. They want us up at the sheriff's station at eleven o'clock."

"I'll be there."

A voice oscilloscope—another product of the electronic age? Lie detectors, too, had been considered infallible when they first appeared; they were being discredited now. As a product of the previous mechanical age, I had a deep, if errant, suspicion of the worth of anything electronic. The TV tube was responsible for that.

At eleven o'clock, in McClune's office, a short, thin officer wearing thick glasses tried to explain to Bernie and me the principles of the oscilloscope.

We both nodded in understanding, though I didn't understand a word of it. I didn't ask Bernie if he did. Bright as he is, he hates to admit he is not as bright as he thinks he is.

What both of us understood was how the machine was to be used.

Bernie had brought Toledo's phone number. A woman officer dialed it. She was, she explained over the phone, a friend of his wife's and she had just had a disturbing phone call from her. The dialogue went on and on, every word being recorded. She would have made a great private eye; she was one beautiful liar.

When she had finished, the tape that had just been recorded and the tape of the anonymous caller were taken by the expert into his private sanctum to be compared.

We all waited in the office, nobody talking, everybody hoping.

About ten minutes later the expert came out and shook his head.

"For sure?" McClune asked.

"For sure," the man said.

"Damn it!" McClune said. "We're back to nowhere!"

"Maybe not," I said. "I have another number you can try."

They all stared at me. McClune asked, "Whose?"

"George Culver's," I said.

"Why? Do you know something we don't?"

"All I have is a hunch. What can we lose?"

"Nothing," he admitted. "You do the calling this time."

There is an old vaudeville adage—never follow a banjo act with another banjo act. Following the previous call would be more like following a concert violinist with a country fiddler.

I shook my head.

"Why not?" McClune asked.

I nodded at the woman. "Because she's better at it."

Vogel said, "Do it, Brock. Nobody lies better than you do."

"Okay," I said. "Give me time to tune my fiddle."

That made as much sense to them as the explanation of how the oscilloscope worked had to me. They said nothing as I composed my opening line.

I thought it was a pretty good one, even if it was borrowed from my predecessor. When Culver answered the phone I said, "This is Brock Callahan, George. I've just had a phone call from Tony Toledo."

"So?"

"The police have learned that the woman Chris was involved with was Mavis Toledo."

"Why should that concern me? For your information, Callahan, Tony and I are not exactly buddies since he went to work for Abbot and Clarke."

"I know. He told me the same thing when I was in his office yesterday. But now the law seems to think he is the number one choice for the murder of Andropolus. He phoned me and suggested I look a little further up the line of command. I had the feeling he meant you."

"You're lying," he said. "What kind of trap are you trying to set?"

"I am trying to find the real killer. That's all I give a damn about. Could I come over this afternoon and talk with you? I have reason to believe your phone is tapped."

"I'll be home," he said. "You had better make more sense than you have so far when you get here."

I cradled the phone and looked around the room. My predecessor smiled at me. "Thank God I'm not married to you," she said.

Into the sanctum with the new tape. I held my thumbs. I was still holding them when the expert came out and nodded.

"For sure?" McClune asked again.

The man nodded.

McClune smiled. Fran smiled. Bernie frowned and said, "What have we got? So far we have doubtful proof that Culver made the phone call. But no proof that he is the killer."

"I object to that first part," the expert said stiffly. "We have much more than *doubtful* proof."

"And," McClune said, "we have reasonable grounds for a search warrant if we can find a judge who's available today."

"I can get us one," Bernie said. "He owes me. But

what do you expect to find? There was no weapon involved."

McClune looked at Fran and Fran at McClune. They both looked embarrassed. Finally, McClune told him about the button and went on quickly to explain that the only reason they hadn't shared it with the city was because of Chief Chandler Harris's big mouth.

Bernie said grudgingly, "I'll buy that—for now. I'll go and get the warrant."

The woman officer smiled at all of us. "I thought this might happen, so I brought a picnic lunch. You can sit next to me, Mr. Callahan."

"You may call me Brock," I told her.

"Only if you'll call me Alice."

Bernie left. I sat next to Alice, giving me first choice on the sandwiches. I rummaged through them. They all had lettuce in them.

"I suppose," she said, "you're like my husband. You hate lettuce."

"No way! I love lettuce!"

She smiled a knowing smile. "I retract my former statement. I lie better than you do."

I considered that a challenge. I chose the leafiest of the sandwiches and bit into it manfully.

Fran and McClune played gin rummy after lunch. Alice asked me why I had suspected Culver.

"Proximity mostly," I explained to her. "The timing required it. And then I realized he was one suspect who had access to the books. He must have noticed the coincidental pattern of the dates Toledo was out of town and Chris pretended to be. He knew about his partner's sexual drive. He also knew that Toledo was their best bet to gain access to the carriage trade—they needed him. He had probably gone over to read the riot act to Chris. They were both hotheads; one word had led to a nastier one—and come to blows. When he realized Chris was dead he saw a chance to take over the operation, divert suspicion from himself, and get rid of an enemy."

"That's brilliant," Alice said. "No wonder you're rich."

I saw no reason to explain to her that that wasn't the reason I was rich. Humility can be overdone.

Fran and Bernie left for the Culver house. McClune told me I was welcome to accompany them, but I declined the invitation. I drove home with the uncomfortable feeling that Ricardo might still be brought to trial. The police hadn't even been able to connect Culver with the chop shop operation. Nor could I believe he was the kind of man who favored British tailoring.

My best hope was the persuasive technique of a Bernard Vogel interrogation. That was not my forte, the main reason I had not gone with them.

I could picture Bernie explaining in his tactful way that if Andropolus had made the first move in the scuffle, Culver could claim self-defense.

I could picture Culver explaining in his larcenous way that that was indeed how it had happened—except there had been no scuffle. Andropolus had become enraged during the argument, started around the desk toward him, stumbled, and fallen into the fatal corner of the desk. He had not known Andropolus was dead when he left.

That was the way I pictured it because that is the way I would have explained it if I had been Culver. But it was only a dream.

Button, button, who's got the button . . . ?

I took a long, warm, massage shower at home and two antiacid tablets. None of Mrs. Casey's daytime dramas were available today; she looked lost. I suggested a game of gin rummy.

It was three o'clock and Mrs. Casey was two dollars and twenty-eight cents into my wallet when Bernie phoned.

The interrogation, he told me, had gone more or less the way I had pictured it—with one minor change in the script. Fran had told Culver that Ricardo had identified Culver's voice from the recording as the same voice he had heard over the phone.

"The damned fool!" I said. "Didn't he realize the DA will learn that was a lie?"

"It was a lie," he admitted. "But we went down to the station from there and Ricardo confirmed it. I wish you had been with us. You lie better than Fran does. But that doesn't matter now. We found the jacket with the missing button and Culver is going with his self-defense plea. He'll have a hard time selling *that* to the DA."

"Thank God!" I said.

"And thank your unerring bloodhound instincts. Stay healthy, Brock. We need you around."

I phoned the Felderstadt apartment and Pete answered. I gave him the good news and he congratulated me.

Then I went back and got a dollar and twelve cents into Mrs. Casey's purse before Jan came home.

If you have enjoyed this book and would like to receive details of other Walker mystery titles, please write to:

Mystery Editor
Walker and Company
720 Fifth Avenue
New York, NY 10019